BILL JAQUETTE

GIDEON'S GRAND-CHILDREN

ARJ Publishing

ISBN (paperback) 978-1-7379328-0-2
ISBN (ebook) 978-1-7379328-1-9

Cover design by Aaxel Author Services
& Noah Adam Paperman
Interior design by Aaxel Author Services

Printed in the United States of America

For my sons, Roger and Adam,
and granddaughter Abby.

CONTENTS

FOREWORD

Much of the world views the public defenders in America as they are represented in *My Cousin Vinny*, as lawyers who graduated at the bottom of their law school class and took the only job open to them. Not so! And I tell you this because I spent almost all my 40 years as an attorney as a public defender. Going to court every day in contests on which the future of a life depends and using every ounce of creativity to win a favorable ruling from the judge or, better yet, a not-guilty verdict from the jury, has attracted lawyers from all levels on the class rankings of every law school.

That better be the way it is. In the early 1960s, Clarence Gideon—that's his picture on the front cover—wrote a handwritten petition from his prison cell to the United States Supreme Court complaining that he hadn't received the "assistance of counsel" when he was convicted of burglary in a Florida court. In so doing, he started something that resulted in a ruling from the Court in Gideon v. Wainwright that the Sixth Amendment to the United States Constitution required that every person charged with a crime be given the assistance of counsel at the expense of the government if they were unable to afford it on their own. From that point on, public defenders—

then Gideon's children, now, almost a half century later, his grandchildren—took up their critical role in the American justice system. Statistics collected in 2007 (most recent data from the Bureau of Justice Statistics) show there were over fifteen thousand lawyers practicing as full-time public defenders handling over five and a half million cases that year, amounting to over 80 percent of all the criminal cases coming before the courts. And those numbers have only grown since. These lawyers did not hang their chance of success on last-minute help from a girlfriend as Vinny Gambini did in *My Cousin Vinny*, but rather on their skillful employment of all the tools of the legal profession.

This is my true story about the lawyers, investigators, social workers, and office assistants in their jobs as public defenders and about their clients. There is no Hudson County Public Defender (HCPD) and the descriptions of the characters and what happens to them are fiction. As a lawyer, what I know about my real clients is confidential, and can't be retold. However, these stories closely represent what does occur because they were pieced together from the multiplicity of real incidents I experienced and those shared with me by my public defender colleagues and my prosecutor adversaries.

The action is played out against the criminal laws of the State of Washington. The court procedures follow those of the Snohomish County Superior Court. And the operations at the HCPD parallels those at of the Snohomish County Public Defender Association, where I worked for 30 of those 40 years. The main character, Steve Cole, would find himself with many differences were he a public defender in another state or even in a different county in Washington. However, criminal laws and the court proceedings used to enforce those laws everywhere arise out of similar histories and serve essentially the same purpose, as does the role of the public defender, ensuring that enforcement is fair. As a result, the roads and barriers encountered at the HCPD do parallel what happens in reality elsewhere.

We hear and read stories about the criminal legal system where a corrupt prosecutor or judge does something that is not in the interest of justice but for a personal gain or to avoid a physical threat or just a political risk. Although not often in a position of power that would invite such corruption, public defense attorneys are not immune to such failures. However, more likely to occur with public defenders is an abandonment of the commitment to the client in favor of an accommodation to the interests of the courts, prosecutors, and all the other interests alive in the criminal courts, often having to do with expediting the overwhelming number of cases the criminal courts have to handle. Most of this results from the insufficient funding suffered by the prosecutors, the courts, and overwhelmingly by the public defenders. There are also many other stories where, historically, intentional racial prejudice and, continuing today, institutional racial biases cause unjust results. For as long as there has been American criminal justice, all forms of prejudice against many forms of identity have caused countless injustices to occur within the criminal justice system. These realities have been well documented in books like Jonathan Rapping's *Gideon's Promise*, Sara Mayeux's *Free Justice*, and Steve Bogira's *Courtroom 302*.

What goes on in the Hudson County courts is certainly not immune from these disorders. The laws and court procedures the HCPD team operate under are, in many ways the products of these problems like anywhere else. However, the focus of this book is not on the corruption, the institutional biases, or the structural problems in the criminal court system. Instead, these stories offer a closeup look, from the vantage point of the public defenders themselves. You will watch what goes on day after day in the work of a better funded—but as you will see, not completely well funded—public defender organization that is fully committed to doing everything possible to help its clients.

The bigger social issues are still all there. Even played against a somewhat theoretical system where the efforts of the public defender are appropriately focused and the other players—the police, prosecutors, and judges—are not corrupt or biased, there is still much to say about what goes on.

Those defense attorneys from TV (like Perry Mason or Ben Matlock) wouldn't have been hired at the HCPD. They only had the skills to handle cases where the client wasn't really guilty and where the real criminal would confess on the witness stand. The cases presented here are fiction, but far from what those TV attorneys experienced, these stories accurately represent what real lawyers, investigators, social workers, and legal assistants encounter in their real work for their clients. The clients of the HCPD aren't real either. However, these stories represent them, even the ones who end up being rightfully convicted of their crimes, not as they are so often portrayed in TV shows like *Law and Order* as trash to be flushed out of the human community, but as real people whose bad decisions have brought them before the court, but whose other qualities are those shared by the rest of us.

—

For the reader interested in just how the law works, the Epilogue presents a short history of the criminal laws in Washington, how they have evolved, and how the current sentencing laws are applied. The effects of these laws on the cases the HCPD team handled are explained in detail.

CHAPTER ONE

No Time to Rest

Cindy Baker and I waited. We had been summoned back to court because the jury had reached a verdict. Cindy was the defendant; she had been charged with first-degree trafficking in stolen property and I was her public defender. My name is Steve Cole—looking at me, the only thing I think that distinguishes me from other males about to turn thirty is the fact that there isn't anything distinguishing about me. I am married with two kids. I love my family and am passionate about my job as a Hudson County Public Defender. For a while, it was just Cindy and me in the courtroom. Anything we could have said to one another had long ago been said, so we sat there in our own thoughts.

We were in the courtroom of Superior Court Judge Dean Jordan in the Hudson County Courthouse in the State of Washington. The courtroom was like every other court in America, not as lavish as some, but all of the elements were there: a jury box where the jury listened to the evidence; a witness box where the witnesses sat and testified; a place for the court staff; an area where the lawyers did their thing; a place where the public could sit and watch the proceedings; and, right out of the middle ages, a station for the judge called the bench, in front of the American and Washington State flags, sitting in the position of power well above the rest of the participants.

We had been in trial for a day and a half. Cindy had been arrested when the police arrived at the house where she and her boyfriend were living. According to the testimony of the witnesses, stolen goods were being purchased by the guy in the house and then resold. The police had been investigating this for some time and had located a couple of "snitches," two of the guys who had been selling their "wares" at the house who had testified in exchange for light sentences to lesser charges. They were willing to say on my cross-examination they had never dealt with Cindy, but they did say they had seen her at the house on a couple of occasions. The police had gotten a search warrant and when they arrived at the house, they found many items that later proved to have been stolen, and Cindy. Her boyfriend was nowhere to be found, and the police were never able to find him.

Cindy seemed a little naïve for her twenty-four years. She had told us she met her boyfriend, Dick Turner, at a bar a year and a half before her arrest, and they had developed a relationship. She was in nursing school with a part-time job and Turner's invitation to move in had helped a lot. It put her near school and her job and did away with the cost of rent. Turner had recently started to get rough with her, but staying there was the only way she would be able to continue in nursing school. Turner had a daytime job, but Cindy had also witnessed people bringing power tools, laptop computers, the occasional TV, jewelry, and other things to the house that Turner then handed over to others. Turner had told her it was a business he had on the side, buying things from friends who wanted to get rid of them and, for a little profit, selling them to people he knew, who were dealers in used merchandise. Cindy said she didn't know any of the stuff had been stolen. I didn't know whether to believe her, but she was pretty young and had no other criminal arrests. Anyway, at this point, it wasn't a question of whether I believed her, but whether the jury would believe us.

The prosecutor, Jack Garner, had not been trying to prove Cindy was trafficking in stolen goods herself, but that she was an accomplice to Mr. Turner, who was. She had to take the stand and tell her story. So, in preparation, she and I had had several sessions where I went over the questions I was going to ask, and another public defender grilled her with the questions we thought the prosecutor was likely to ask. She was as ready as she could be when she took the stand, but terribly frightened. Cindy handled direct examination well. During cross-examination, I had moments of high anxiety when the prosecutor was able to lead her into admitting some things that weren't helpful to us, but she handled most of it pretty well and we got to straighten out a few of the mistakes on my redirect examination.

In my closing argument to the jury, I claimed there was no evidence Cindy knew what Mr. Turner had been up to, but even if the jury concluded she did, that knowledge would not be enough to make her an accomplice. I pointed out there would have to be evidence, proving beyond a reasonable doubt that she assisted in his project, or stood ready to assist, and that this was not what the evidence showed.

The two of us didn't have to wait long. Gardner arrived and took his seat. The judge's law clerk looked out from the judge's chambers and saw us waiting. Soon thereafter, the court staff entered and took their places. Judge Jordan entered, and we all rose and remained standing as the jury came in.

The law clerk walked over and took the verdict form from the presiding juror, passed it to the judge who read it to himself, then passed it to the court clerk to be read into the record.

All the while, Cindy's anxiety level was going through the roof. I was thinking about how this moment was going to affect the rest of her life. Among other things, with a felony conviction, she would have to wait five years from the end of her sentence, including any probation, before she could get that nursing license she'd been working so hard to get. As always at these moments, my anxiety level rose some as well. I looked over my shoulder into the public seating and saw Rachel Pierce, the lawyer that had helped with the practice cross-examination, and a couple of other fellow public defenders, George Sanders and Laura Berg. We always like to be there for support, if we can, when one of us gets a verdict.

Cindy and I stood at the request from the judge and faced the jury as the court clerk read the verdict: "We the jury find the defendant Cindy Baker not guilty of the crime of trafficking in stolen property in the first degree."

I looked at Cindy and saw her beginning to tear up and gestured for her to sit down. I could feel the muscles in my shoulders relax and I took a deep breath. After each of the jurors was asked to confirm this was their individual verdict, they were returned to the jury room and Judge Jordan then addressed himself to Cindy.

"Ms. Baker, the jury has returned a verdict of not-guilty. I will enter findings to that effect and an order dismissing this case. Good luck to you.

"We are in recess."

The judge left the bench, and the courtroom began to clear. My colleagues headed out and, although there was still a little bit more left in the workday, nothing had to be said. We all knew there would be a celebration at the pub after work. Cindy was sitting in her chair and beginning to relax. She'd called her mother when we were told there was a verdict, and the mother was on her way from Tacoma to take her home. I took her into the hall to await her mother and returned to the courtroom to see if any of the jurors wanted to talk.

Most of the jurors didn't pay any attention to Garner and me as they walked out. One of the women on the jury did come up to the two of us and said she thought my client had been lucky and she needed to be more careful in choosing her next boyfriend. That statement from the juror and the fact the other jurors walked away without eye contact led me to conclude the jury probably didn't fully believe Cindy but did take seriously the judge's instruction to "presume the defendant was innocent" and that a guilty verdict required "proof beyond a reasonable doubt."

Garner and I shook hands and left the courtroom. Cindy was there in the hall with her mother. I congratulated her and told her what the juror had said. Cindy said she agreed with her and told me one of our social workers had helped her to find some local temporary housing while the trial was pending and also helped her to apply for some additional financial aid from the school so she could afford student housing. Her mother was also going to help a bit more with the funding as well.

Public defenders always like to go to trial and get a not-guilty verdict. Part of it is the simple satisfaction of winning, but the more important part is the confirmation that we did a good job. More times than not, we do not win our trials, good job or not, and must rightfully accept the disappointment of losing. Having a win every now and again, however, does reinforce our efforts to keep trying to do that "good job." This win was particularly rewarding to me because Cindy might well have actually been innocent and there is reason to think she wouldn't make that next mistake as so many of my other clients do.

———

I hurried back to the office to see how far the day and a half of trial, and the hours spent in preparation for it, had put me behind on all my other cases. I had several cases with trial dates coming up in the next few weeks needing attention and a handful of pretrial defense motions needing to be prepared. Washington has a court rule limiting a public defender attorney's caseload to one hundred and fifty felony cases over the course of a year. If you do the math, that means you get about three felony cases a week, cases with charges anywhere from simple possession of an illegal drug to murder. Sitting on my desk with all the case files I knew about were the files for my three new cases, and I was anxious to see what had been loaded onto my plate. In this day and age, we also have emails and voice and text messages which, with my time away at trial, were now mounting up overwhelmingly.

To try to get a handle on all of this, my first stop was the office of my legal assistant, Polly Jones. Legal assistants are responsible for keeping our calendars up-to-date and helping us to communicate with the prosecutors, court staff, and clients. Polly's first job was in the home where she raised of her four children. At some point in her middle years, her two daughters and two sons started taking care of themselves, and she went looking for another way to be helpful — and found us. I could not survive without all the help she provides. However, her greatest help to me was communicating with my clients. If I was not in my office—and I was often away—Polly answered the calls. Instead of just giving a quick answer, she took the time to engage the clients in conversation, really listening to what they wanted to say, and in the process, developing an insight that helped me better understand the person I was representing. Stepping into her office was like being invited into her home. Some Native American artwork reflected part of her heritage and there were pictures of her children and grandchild at various ages, as well as two large house plants thriving beneath those strange colored grow lights.

As I entered, Polly jumped up and gave me a big hug of congratulations.

"I thought you might have a winner. Cindy just got trapped when she moved in with that guy." Polly knew all about Cindy's case because I had spent a lot of time thinking my way through it with her assistance.

I told her I wanted to get out of there soon and join the celebration at the pub. But I did want to figure out "what's hot," so I could hit the deck running the next day. Polly told me she had my calendar up to date with no court appearances the next day. "The only thing I would highlight is one of your new clients, Jeffrey Harris. He was arraigned last week on a second-degree assault for strangling his wife. He's in custody and has been calling—demanding to see you. He seems to think they should not be holding him because he 'really didn't do anything wrong.' I told him you were in trial, but that didn't seem to satisfy him."

I agreed to see Mr. Harris the next day and headed across the street to the pub to celebrate. There is always a happy hour celebration after work every Friday, but it is not uncommon that a special get together happens other days of the week to celebrate a court victory, or to console someone for a defeat. Two of the lawyers and one of our social workers were already there, and they had a beer waiting for me. I sat down to a short round of applause and explained that this not-guilty verdict was a particular relief because the client might have really been innocent.

I turned to thank social worker Meredith Hayward. She is one of three social workers employed at HCPD. It was she who helped Cindy to find that temporary housing and work through the process for getting the financial aid from the college. Our staff of social workers is always overwhelmed with cases. When you think about it, we should probably have as many social workers as lawyers working at HCPD. Almost all our clients have some kind of problem in addition to their criminal charges and were in need of help: housing, employment, physical problems, mental health, drugs and more. One of the great advantages we have is our social workers can operate within the same realm of confidentiality as the lawyers have and get to the bottom of the client's social problem more effectively than a social worker from an outside agency who'd have to turn over negative information to the authorities.

Meredith was more interested in another one of my clients,

Gilbert Martin. She told me she thought he was incompetent to stand trial. Gilbert had a history of mental illness, but when I had interviewed him, he seemed to have a good grasp of what was going on with his case. Apparently, when Meredith talked to him, the conversation got more fanciful, leading her to conclude there were some serious delusions hiding at the core of his thinking. I decided I'd better add him to my jail visits the next day. It would be unfair for him to go to trial and exhibit some strange thinking not connected with reality during his testimony.

My list of things to do the next day was growing, but it had become time to relax and enjoy the company of my fellow warriors. A large contingent of people from the office had arrived by then, drinks were ordered, and many conversations begun. There was talk about all sorts of things, some outrageous thing a prosecutor had done, a decision a judge had made, a difficult client to work with, the idiot another lawyer was dating, and how the Seahawks were doing this season. The HCPD Director, Jill Zimmerman, had joined us and at one point rose to offer a toast to congratulate me for my not-guilty verdict and another attorney Anita Carter, for winning an argument at a pretrial hearing resulting in the court ordering the evidence to be suppressed, which meant the prosecutor would have to dismiss the case. It was a happy time and everything of consequence could wait until the next day.

—

I had been working at HCPD for five years. My mother and father are both lawyers. They worked together in a law firm in partnership with three other lawyers. My mother had a civil business practice, and my father did estate planning. I was always going to be a lawyer and, hopefully, someday become a partner with my parents. I made it through law school easily, helped in part because my parents always knew the answers to the questions

I had. During law school, mostly for the entertainment value, I participated in an internship at a public defender office where I got to represent some of the public defender clients in court on misdemeanor charges. I even got to try one case to a jury, with my supervisor sitting right beside me, of course. I lost the case badly, and my supervisor had a long list of mistakes I had made.

However, when it came to look for a real job, I couldn't let go of that internship experience. At that point, I knew I would only do it for two years, but I hired on as one of the lawyers at HCPD. For the person I think I had become, this proved to be the perfect job. I hate to admit it, but I was attracted by all the action, all the legal tussling with the prosecutors and sometimes with the judges, not on behalf of some abstract social interest, but on behalf of a single person who may well have done what the prosecutor was accusing them of doing but still deserved my help. Those two years became five, with no plans to leave.

—

Infused by the not-guilty verdict and a restful night's sleep, I stopped at the office to pick up files and headed to the jail. Polly had arranged for me to meet with several of my clients. First on my list was Gilbert Martin, the guy Meredith and I had talked about at the pub. When he arrived at the interview room, he was in handcuffs. The guards accompanying him told me he had been having trouble in the regular unit and got moved into segregation. They uncuffed him and walked away. Gilbert entered the interview room and sat down across the table from me, and the door was locked shut.

At my first conference with Gilbert, we had had a long and useful discussion about his case and what to do in response to the charges. On this occasion, it took him a little while to remember who I was, and he was hesitating in his responses to my questions.

Sometimes, when a client with mental health problems is put in jail, away from the support they had in the community, their mental health deteriorates. It looked like this was what had happened, and it explained the experience Meredith had when she went to see him. We had tried to get him released into his mother's care, but the mother had felt, with the state of her health, she couldn't take on the responsibility at this time. So, Gilbert just had to sit it out in jail.

Gilbert had been charged with second-degree robbery. He'd gone into a Safeway, filled his bag with food and walked out without paying. Two store employees pursued him. When they caught up with him and grabbed ahold of his arms, he pushed them away, waved his fist in the air in a threatening manner, and ran away, only to be caught by the police still running with the stolen goods two blocks from the store. All these facts would have been easily proved by the prosecutor. There was nothing we could do if we took the case to trial, unless we could show Gilbert was insane or had a diminished mental capacity. The prosecutor had offered to reduce the charge to a misdemeanor theft with a sentence of thirty days if he'd plead guilty. In our earlier conversation, Gilbert had wanted to take that deal, which would have had him out in another two weeks.

The way Gilbert was responding to me was confirming Meredith's concern about his competency. But if we had gone down that road to investigate his competency, we'd have had to stop the legal proceedings and put him on a waiting list to be visited by a psychologist from the state mental hospital. Waiting for his place on the hospital's schedule would have kept him in jail all the time he'd serve with the guilty plea before he was even seen by the psychologist. If he were then found incompetent to stand trial, he'd have continued to remain in the jail until there was a bed available at the mental hospital for which there was also a long waiting list. Once at the hospital, he'd go into treatment until he was made competent, at which time he'd be returned to the jail, and we could then proceed to deal with his charges. All of this would keep him in custody at least four or five times as long as he would spend with his plea deal, and even longer than if he had been convicted and sentenced for the original robbery charge.

It is almost always the defense attorney who first notices a defendant who might be incompetent to stand trial because they are the ones working directly with them during the court proceedings. If the attorney expresses to the court any doubt about the client's competency, the judge will invariably set the evaluation process in play. I wanted to be sure of what to do before I said anything to the court.

A person is incompetent to stand trial if, "as a result of a mental disease or defect," they don't have "the capacity to understand the nature of the proceedings" or the capacity to "assist in (their) own defense." I began by asking Gilbert if he knew what he was charged with, what my role was as his attorney, what a prosecutor was, and what a judge was. He seemed occasionally to get distracted as he responded but was able to answer all those questions correctly. He also knew what a jury did and what would happen if he were found guilty. Gilbert clearly understood the "nature of the proceedings." The harder thing to determine was whether a defendant could "assist in his defense." This is where delusional thinking can impair competency. Gilbert gave a clear history of what had happened at the Safeway. However, he could not explain why he walked out of the store without paying. While I am no expert on mental illness, it seemed clear to me some distorted thinking was involved because he had walked out of the store so boldly in front of several store employees.

I began to ask him about other things in his life. He was residing with his mother, living on social security disability payments because of his mental illness, and receiving therapy at a community mental health center. Getting back to that situation, perhaps with some assistance for his mother, would be best. We talked again about the prosecutor's plea offer. He had to understand the conviction would go on his record, and he would also have to serve a period of probation, which the judge could revoke if he screwed up again, then give him up to 334 more days in jail. He told me he understood and wanted to take the deal to get out of jail.

The urgency of anyone waiting in jail for their case to be resolved so they can get out of jail has made even some of the most rational people make the wrong decision about their case. So, I needed something more. I told Gilbert the judge was going to need to know he was thinking straight in making this decision.

"Mr. Cole, I've been mentally ill almost all my life, and I have come to know when I am not thinking straight. I have been thinking about this quite a bit and I know the best thing for me will be to get out of jail, live with my mother, and get back into treatment. I need to take this plea deal."

That satisfied me. The plea deal was Gilbert's best option, and his decision to take it was being freely and intelligently made. I would set him on the court calendar[1] for a guilty plea as soon as I could schedule it and see if Meredith could find some social services to help him and his mother at home.

—

Gilbert's case had taken a lot longer than I had planned. Not much more of the morning remained. However, Polly had made it clear I had to see Jeff Harris.

The man who walked into the interview room was tall and fit, but from the prominent scar on his forehead and obvious surgery

---

[1] A Court's Calendar is a list of cases the court will be considering during a particular court session. When a lawyer wishes the court to consider an issue in one of their cases, they will seek to schedule it on the Court's Calendar.

on his left arm, he appeared to have been in some sort of accident. He was quite angry, perhaps even angrier because he had been removed from his living unit to sit in a holding cell all morning waiting for me. I felt a little intimidated.

"Mr. Harris, I am your lawyer, Stephen Cole."

"Well, it's about time."

I apologized for the delay and told him, knowing it probably wasn't going to satisfy him, I'd been in trial. Although he had already read the police reports, he demanded I explain why he was in jail for this thing. Again, telling him something I knew he knew, I explained he had been charged with second-degree assault for strangling his wife.

"But Darlene didn't get hurt," he replied, still angry.

I responded that Washington has a fairly new law making it a second-degree assault to compress someone's neck to obstruct the flow of blood or the ability to breathe.

"But that never happened."

"Mr. Harris, you are here because your wife told the police it did."

"So, this is going to be like all my other cases where a lousy public defender helps me to plead guilty and I get hauled off to prison."

Jeff continued to be angry, and I had to control myself not to respond in kind. Many of our clients start off with little faith in their public defender attorney because of the way public defenders are so often portrayed. However, I can't help but get my back up when anyone, including one of my clients, appears to be buying into that kind of thinking.

It is certainly true the time pressure from the large number of cases a public defender is forced to take—necessitated by the limited public funding—makes them look for the shortcuts. That was one of the things that made me question taking this job. Fortunately, there are caseload limits for public defenders in

Washington and I knew because I was a part of it that the lawyers and everybody else at HCPD work vigorously and effectively representing their clients.

I'd noticed Jeff had entered guilty pleas in all his earlier cases, but that didn't mean he hadn't been properly represented. A large majority of the criminal cases going through the courts in America, with good lawyers and bad, end as guilty pleas. However, that is certainly something which might make Jeff think he hadn't been well represented. Another thing, of course, he'd been sitting in jail for a week without getting to see me. I had to find a way to work with him. I promised him we were going to get working hard on his case and do everything legally possible to help him. The first thing on Jeff's agenda was a bail hearing so he could get out of jail and find work.

Jeff calmed down a little when we began planning for the bail hearing. He couldn't go home if he was released because of a no-contact order the court had imposed between him and his family. However, we needed to get his wife's agreement for him to be out of custody. We decided to check with his brother Bill to see if Jeff could stay with him. Jeff suggested we also talk to the employer where he would have started work the day after he was arrested, and a couple of his buddies he thought would say favorable things. I told Jeff his criminal record was probably going to be our biggest barrier to his being released, but succeed or not, I was hopeful a good effort on my part at the bail hearing would give Jeff some confidence we'd be doing everything possible to help him.

I wanted to talk about what Jeff was facing. The range of confinement for most felony sentences in Washington is set on the basis of the type of crime charged and the number and type of the defendant's prior convictions. When I began to talk about his sentence range, Jeff's frustration was re-ignited.

"Here you go again pushing me along to plead guilty."

"Mr. Harris, that is not my intent, but there are a number

of decisions you are going to have to make, including whether to plead guilty for which you will need to know the possible consequences." I told him the prosecutor sent me a report showing convictions for two counts of burglary in Missouri and two counts of vehicular homicide here in Washington. Jeff confirmed there was nothing else. The report had identified the Missouri cases as just burglaries. Jeff told me he and some buddies had broken into some stores and stolen things as teenagers. I told him that meant his sentence range would most likely be 43 to 57 months in prison.

Still hostile. "That is completely ridiculous. I know I frightened Darlene, but I didn't hurt her."

"Jeff, it comes out that way because of your criminal record. If this were your first felony offense, you'd be looking at a range of three to nine months. What moves it up so high are your prior convictions."

"But what about the fact that those crimes occurred a long time ago? The last conviction was in two thousand three and I have been out of prison for over nine years without even a speeding ticket."

"None of that affects the calculus setting the sentence range. Those are things we can say to the judge if you get convicted, and something we can use in negotiating with the prosecutor about the charges."

"Here we go again, talking plea. I didn't do anything, and I should not be spending any time in jail."

"Let me work on it. We will never give up your right to a trial and if we go to trial, we will do everything possible to get you an acquittal. We are going to get you on for that bail hearing, and I will get one of our investigators to interview the witnesses. You need to hang in there."

I hit the button, the guards came and took Jeff back to his unit, and I went to get lunch.

CHAPTER TWO

It All Starts Here

I was scheduled to handle the one o'clock video court. Hudson County Superior Court holds a video court once each day of the week at one o'clock. This is an opportunity for the court to deal with various matters involving defendants who are in jail. Instead of bringing the defendants from the jail across the county campus to the courthouse, the defendants and their attorneys in the jail "go to court" electronically over a video system to the real courtroom where the judge and prosecutor operate.

In addition to our work on the individual assigned cases, the lawyers at HCPD have a regular schedule of court hearings where they stand in on relatively simple matters in cases assigned to the other lawyers. It would be better if we could each be there with all our own clients in this first appearance in court and every appearance thereafter, but, given the heavy caseloads everyone has, this arrangement gives us more time to concentrate on the complicated issues in our cases. The one o'clock video court was one of those extra duties, and it was my turn to cover it. Most of the cases are arraignments where the defendants learn what crime they are being charged with, are asked to enter a plea — at this stage it is always not-guilty — and are told how much bail they would have to post in order to be out of custody while their case is pending. There are always a few defendants with other things to be decided by the court as well.

Robin Chambers was going to help me. She is another legal assistant. She was hired right out of high school and, although I don't recognize those celebrities she likes to talk about, her youthful enthusiasm always made her a pleasure to work with. Robin wasn't assigned to assist individual lawyers with their cases like Polly, but rather to manage general office responsibilities. She spent that morning getting the list from the court of the cases to be heard and gathering all the information available on the people we would represent. She also helped me at video court itself, where she was the first person from the defense team with face-to-face new client contact, handing out the court papers and obtaining contact information we'd need for the work defending them.

It's a short distance from our offices to the jail, so Robin and I walked over together. From the outside, our county jail looks friendly enough, and we have almost always treated in a friendly manner by the people there to make it work. As we proceeded, however, the electronic search of our bags and bodies, the check-in to get our temporary admission badges, and the heavy steel doors unlocked electronically by somebody we never see, only after we are viewed waiting at the door — all provided an effective reminder of where we were. On our way in, we passed a series of busy stations where wives/husbands, boyfriends/girlfriends, mothers/fathers, kids, and just friends, no longer able to have direct contact with the inmate, now communicated over a telephone and video.

Once through the steel doors, Robin and I walked past the interview rooms, where lawyers were having private face-to-face discussions with their clients. We passed one where an inmate sat waiting for his attorney. I recognize him as a previous client for whom I'd gotten a pretty good plea deal. I couldn't remember his name right then, but when he saw me, he waved.

"Hi Mr. Cole, Rachel Pierce is my lawyer this time around. Is she any good?"

"You bet; I think she is great. What are you here for this time?"

"Stolen credit card."

"Good luck, man."

With that, we walked to the room where we waited for our clients to arrive. Except for the State and US flags on one wall and the audio, video, and other electronic equipment, the room didn't look anything like a courtroom. The walls were the standard cement block painted a pale green, like every other room in the jail. It wasn't long before the inmates entered in single file in their green and white striped uniforms and took their seats, the numerous men on one side of the room and the few women on the other.

During the short time before the judge appeared on the television, Robin went about meeting with clients individually and I spent the time telling the group what was going to happen when the judge called their name. However, I also warned them about keeping silent.

"Except in private with your lawyer, don't talk to anyone about your case. What you say to your lawyer is confidential and can't be used against you in court. Other than that, anything you say can turn into testimony against you. Don't talk to the police. If you have already said something to a police officer, you and your lawyer will just have to figure a way to live with it, but don't say anything more. If you have something to say you think could help prove you're innocent, you and your lawyer can make your statement later after you learn what evidence the prosecutor has against you. You also need to know everything said on the jail phones is recorded, so you can't even talk to your friends or family about your case. If you say something about your case to a girlfriend or your mother, they could become witnesses against you at your trial. Finally, don't talk about your case with others in jail. Not everyone would do it, but there are people in here who'd be very happy to tell the cops what you told them about your case to get themselves a deal on their case."

Everyone who handles video court makes the same speech, so it is a little surprising how many times a client forced to wait in jail for their trial will go ahead and say something over the phone to their mother or girlfriend/boyfriend or to their "jail buddy" that ends up being used against them in trial or ends up being the final reason to give up the trial and plead guilty. Some of the lawyers at HCPD put it off to client stupidity. I think not knowing how the system works is a part of it. But another part is a lack of trust in the system, which comes down to the part the defense lawyers play. So, a really important element of our job is to do everything we can to gain and maintain the trust of their clients.

One of the defendants asked: "I've been talking to my lawyer about my case on the phone; is that recorded too?"

Remembering there had been cases where recorded attorney/client conversations had been intercepted by a police detective more interested in getting a conviction than following the law, I answered: "Those calls are recorded but there is a law against them being used against you. I would, nevertheless, save talking about the facts of your case until you were alone with your lawyer." As I said that, I notice several nodding heads reflecting the not unusual feelings about the protection of the law—or lack of it.

About then, Judge Lawrence Greenberg and the prosecutor, Keith White, appeared on the television and the first case was called. I wasn't the only lawyer in the room. The others were there to appear in only one case, so they went first. Private lawyer Joan Steinberg, who does a lot of criminal cases, all for a remarkably high fee, got her case called first and she was well prepared. Her client was charged with driving while intoxicated and because the client had been convicted of a number of DUIs in the past, his current charge was a felony with a long prison sentence if he got convicted. The defendant pled not guilty, and then Steinberg argued for his release. In preparation for the hearing, she had confirmed her client could live with his grandmother and had already arranged for an in-patient alcohol treatment program. Judge Greenberg reduced the bail from the twenty thousand dollars, which the prosecutor had requested, to ten thousand dollars. That defendant could have posted the twenty thousand dollars, but the reduction helped him in paying the rest of Steinberg's legal fees. Seeing how effective a lawyer can be in this circumstance when armed with the necessary information made me a little embarrassed about the minimal extent of the presentations I was going to be able to make. Defendants with resources are usually more likely to be released. They have more opportunities on the outside likely to convince the judge to release them. Nevertheless, the difference between the quality of our client's experience in front of the judge and that of Steinberg's client did not go unnoticed.

Public defender George Sanders, whose office was next to mine, had one case. His client had been arraigned a couple of days earlier but denied a bail reduction at that time. George had obtained verification of a place for his client to live and a job opportunity and had talked to the prosecutor assigned to the case into agreeing to a release. That defendant had only a couple of prior misdemeanor convictions and was only facing a theft charge, so the judge agreed to a release without bail.

Laura Berg was there with another public defender client who had a tougher case. Her client Joe Sellers was charged with an assault; had a prior felony conviction; had failed to appear for court several times in the past; and White was not agreeing to a release. Nevertheless, Laura had a plan for him, which included some personal counseling and a place to live away from the complaining witness. Laura even offered that her client could post a reduced bail of five thousand dollars. Unfortunately, that road was still too steep, and Judge Greenberg denied the reduction of bail.

I was to handle the rest of the cases. The jail guards asked me to take one particular case first. When we first arrived at the jail courtroom, Robin and I could hear someone yelling and banging on a door in one of the holding cells. When the guards made that request, I figured that was the guy they were talking about. Ben Strong was brought in, in handcuffs and leg shackles, with two guards standing close by. At our request, the judge gave me a few minutes to talk to Ben. I pushed the button, turning off the microphone and faced him. Our conversation did not go far before I became concerned about his competency to stand trial. I never did understand what he was talking about, but it wasn't about his plea to the charge or not talking about his case with anyone but his lawyer. At my request, the judge set the case over to the next day. Before then, his newly assigned public defender would talk to him in private and, at the next hearing, either have him enter his not-guilty plea and proceed with the case or ask the judge to set the case on for a competency evaluation.

Most of the other cases were simple. I had nothing to argue, and Judge Greenberg orally advised the defendants of their charges and set the amount of bail White had asked for. The hope was that the defendants' assigned lawyers could develop some information, as George and Laura had done with their clients today, to lead to better results the next time those defendants went to court.

At this stage, every defendant is strongly urged to enter a plea of not guilty. It is far too early in the process to be entering a plea of guilty. There was so much more to consider. Some prosecutors in other counties condition their offer of a plea-deal on a guilty-plea from the defendant at arraignment. That idea had been suggested by the Hudson County Prosecutor but rejected by us and the county judges. Now, if there is to be a plea-deal, the defendant will be given time to consider all of the factors with their lawyer.

The next case was Penny Kartman—charged with identity theft for trying to use a stolen credit card. Her case was particularly memorable to me because I had seen so many "Pennys" here under these same circumstances: a very young woman; charged with some version of theft; looking completely overwhelmed— hair in a mess and open sores on her face, indicating abuse of methamphetamine. Penny wanted me to ask for her release and, with her only prior convictions misdemeanors, she had looked like a good candidate under the usual court standards. Her mother had showed up in the courtroom, and Penny was hoping her mother would support her. Unfortunately for the daughter, her mother provided the judge with tales of Penny's drug use and association with people the mother claimed were "criminals," and the release was quickly denied by the judge. Because I was representing Penny, it was my duty to argue for what she wanted. However, her mother was probably right, just releasing her would have just sent her back to her druggy buddies. Keeping her in custody at this point would give her public defender and one of our social workers an opportunity to work with her setting up a treatment option to which she, by then, would be willing to commit.

The next case involved charges in another state, a fugitive case. Aaron Damborg was charged with a theft by the State of Kansas. When he hadn't appeared for his arraignment there, the judge in Kansas issued a warrant. Aaron had come to Washington to spend some time with his father and when stopped by the police for a dead taillight in his father's car, the police saw the warrant on their computer and arrested him. The court in Washington has some control over the process, but ultimately must honor Kansas' demand for the defendant. The judge in Kansas had asked for bail of fifty thousand dollars, far more than any judge around here would set for a simple theft crime and far more than Aaron and his father could afford. We asked that bail be set at five thousand dollars, arguing the defendant had no prior convictions, and he was in Washington visiting his father and wouldn't have known that charges had been filed in Kansas. Judge Greenberg said he wouldn't reduce the bail the Kansas judge had imposed without further information and set the next court date. If we couldn't find a way around it, a special bus for transporting fugitives, and any others needing to be moved to a different jail, would pick him up and drive from jail to jail, picking up and delivering others along the route, stopping for the night to house him and the rest of the "cargo" in a convenient jail, and finally delivering him to Kansas. All I could do was tell Aaron his assigned public defender would be visiting soon to see what could be done.

Rory Cookson, the next defendant up, arrived angry. When asked by the judge what his plea was, he loudly responded "not guilty." He had quite a record of prior convictions and court dates he had missed. As Rory had requested, I asked the judge to release him, but Rory immediately broke in and started telling the judge he didn't commit that crime and that the judge had to release him. Judge Greenberg, citing to his criminal record, denied Rory's release, and set the bail at what White had asked.

"Well, fuck you judge!"

I hit the button to turn off the microphone to avoid any more grounds for finding Rory in contempt of court. The jail guards moved in, pulled Rory away, handed him his court paperwork, and took him back to his housing unit. It occurred to me, having seen Rory's behavior, that some of the other defendants, now forced to sit here until the court session ended, regretted they too hadn't sworn at the judge to get an early trip back to their living units.

Alan Thomas had a criminal record as bad as Cookson's. He pled "not guilty" to the charges and, like Cookson, interrupted me as I started to ask for his release. However, the difference was like night and day.

"Your Honor, I know my record doesn't look good, but when I got out of prison last November, I promised myself I would turn things around. I have a job and I joined a group of former prisoners who get together to help one another when things go wrong. I really need to stay out of jail to keep things on the right path."

Judge Greenberg was taken by Alan's sincerity and let him go.

The defendant in the next case was one of Rachel Pierce's clients, Lila Daniels. She had failed to appear at court on the date of her trial. Rachel couldn't be in court to represent her but sent me an email with the details of what had happened. When called, Lila joined me in front of the camera. I asked the court to release her and began to relate the information Rachel had provided.

"Your Honor, Ms. Daniels lives east of here, up in the mountains. She had scheduled a ride with her boyfriend to court for her trial call, but about the time the boyfriend was to show up at the door, he called and told her he couldn't start his truck. She then had tried to get her father to take her, but the father had to get to work that morning in the other direction. Ms. Daniels did call her lawyer, Ms. Pierce, before she was to appear, and Ms. Pierce related this to Judge Jordan, who was presiding at trial call.

"Judge Jordan did issue a bench warrant but said he would consider the client's excuses when Ms. Daniels again appeared in court. Ms. Daniels told me how she'd continued trying to arrange for a ride, but the boyfriend's truck was not going to be easily fixed and the father's employer had refused to give him time off to help her. She'd finally flagged down a deputy sheriff a couple of days later to turn herself in and was brought to jail."

"Your Honor, that story is simply not believable," White responded. "That here in the twenty-first century a person can't arrange for a timely ride just can't be true. If nothing else, Ms. Daniels could just have grabbed her cellphone and have an Uber driver at her door in a matter of minutes."

"Your Honor, counsel is ignoring the fact the defendant lives in a small community where, even if an Uber driver would come out that far, it would probably take several hours for them to get there, and Uber costs a lot of money. In any event, Ms. Pierce could attest to receiving the defendant's call prior to the time of the trial-call hearing and the arrest report does confirm Ms. Daniels did turn herself in. The defendant is charged with identity theft one, but she is at this point presumed innocent. She has no felony convictions and her only other failure to appear in court was at the arraignment on this charge for which she did not have actual notice."

"Mr. Cole," said Judge Greenberg, "I am not going to completely discount your client's story. I can imagine transportation emergencies do occur, and I don't think Uber would be in a position to provide a quick remedy. However, I think timely transportation could have been arranged. This case must proceed to a resolution and your client has missed court twice. I am going to lower the bail from $10,000, but I am going to set it at $5,000. I think we need that extra incentive for her to be in court."

Daniels spoke up, "Sir, my family can't post that much bail."

"I've made my ruling."

Daniels then turned to me. "I just want to plead guilty."

The judge's offer of a compromised had been no compromise at all because it would still cost money Lila and her father just didn't have, and I was pretty sure that Judge Greenberg wasn't so naïve as to really expect that they would have it. The result was that the case created a circumstance where Lila would either have to plead guilty or spend more time in jail waiting for her trial than she would spend serving the sentence if convicted. I told her that Rachel would be over to see her soon to help her decide what to do. Lila walked away, crying. One more time where the interests of efficient court proceedings trumped the circumstances of the individual.

With that, we were done. Robin and I packed up all the paperwork we had generated in the hearings and walked down the hall, past a room with ten men crowded together waiting for their lawyer visit, then past a second room with not quite as many women waiting for their lawyer visits. At the big steel door, I buzzed to be released and when identified by "that someone you never see," the latch clicked, and we were out.

CHAPTER THREE

All in a Day's Work

The schedule for every criminal court will always include a hearing somewhere between the arraignment and the day of trial, where the prosecution and defense appear in court under the supervision of the judge to figure out what decisions will have to be made in advance of trial so the trial could proceed efficiently. In the superior courts in the State of Washington, these are called Omnibus Hearings. With the increasing number of cases coming through the courts over the last few decades, what used to be an opportunity for some real decisions about cases has become a thirty second stopover for the great herd of defendants marching through on the way to their trial or, way more often, a guilty plea.

On this day, 85 cases were scheduled for court in a session slated to last an hour and a half. I was there along with many other public defenders, several prosecutors, and several defense lawyers in private practice. Defendants who were not in jail, often in the company of their family or friends, filled the public seating, with the overflow lined up against the wall. A room in the back was filled with those defendants being held in jail. Early in the morning, they had been moved from their living units into a holding cell, where they waited, then were led in chains to the court through an underground walkway for their thirty seconds before the judge.

The judge had not yet taken the bench, which gave the defense attorneys an opportunity to talk with their clients and negotiate with the prosecutors. In a better world, these conversations would have been held in advance outside the courtroom, but with all the cases coming through the system, neither side had the time to be that prepared.

I had four clients scheduled that day. Two were in custody and I had been over to the jail to talk to them both. Debra King was charged with attempting to elude. She had been driving her neighbor's 5-year-old son home from school when she saw a police officer attempting to pull her over. Realizing she had lost her license from a recent DUI conviction (her second), she attempted to get away racing through a school zone where children were out playing, but all happily off the street. When stopped, her blood test showed her under the influence of opiates. Debra wanted to plead guilty but with multiple charges available to the prosecutor and several probation violations pending, we had some negotiating to do, so the prosecutor and I agreed just to move the case along and talk later.

Ray Langus was charged with second-degree robbery. The prosecutor had brought him back from prison, where he was already serving a sentence for two other robberies, to face charges for a third. This new robbery had been committed between the times of the other two. This charge hadn't been filed along with the other two because the police report had been sitting on the police department's out-box and then the prosecutor's in-box while the other two were being dealt with in court. Ray just wanted to plead guilty and get back to prison. By being brought back to jail, he had been dropped out of drug treatment and a college class he was taking. He and I had looked at the witness statements for the case, and it looked rock solid for the prosecutor. Keith White was the prosecutor in the case. He and I agreed to set it on for a guilty plea and sentencing at the same time and luckily there was space that afternoon to facilitate Ray's wish.

I had yet to see my two clients who were not in custody. We always send letters to out-of-custody clients urging them to call or come in to schedule an appointment with their lawyers. Some do and some don't. Neither of these clients of mine had done that, so I was just hoping they'd show up. It always works better when defendants come to court. However, I can appreciate their reticence to do so. It is kind of like if I had an appointment to have my foot cut off.

The conversations stopped momentarily, and everyone stood when Judge Dennis Armstrong walked in. Judge Armstrong is a decent fellow when you meet him off the bench, willing to joke around with all the lawyers appearing regularly before him. But like many of his brethren, infused with the power of the law when he takes the bench, he becomes a fire-breathing commander-in-chief.

"Be seated. I see we have 85 cases to be heard today. I expect everyone to be ready when their case gets called. I waited an extra ten minutes before coming out here and that should have been enough time for everyone to be ready."

With that, the judge began to call the cases in the order listed. With our voices low so as not to disturb the proceedings, several of my fellow public defenders and I walked along the public seating looking for our yet-to-arrive clients. I stepped forward with Lori and Ray when their cases were called and in their thirty seconds each and without discussion, the judge signed the agreed orders for their cases. I then returned on the prowl for my two other clients.

The court proceedings were not going well. The judge's expectations were not being fulfilled. Several times, a case was not ready when it was called, and it had to be "footed" to the end of the list. The whole room could see the judge was getting frustrated and finally, in a raised voice: "This is not the way things are supposed to go. We have only so much time this morning to get through these cases, and there are going to be consequences where cases are not ready when they are called."

There were, of course, reasons why we weren't ready. For some, it was because the prosecutor and defense attorney hadn't had a chance to talk about the case, but for most, it was either because the defense lawyer and client were just meeting for the first time and needed to talk, or because the client still hadn't showed.

One of the prosecutors, Beth Wilkerson, came up to me looking for Howard Graham, one of the lawyers at HCPD. She pointed to a man sitting with a friend in the third row and told me that was Jack O'Reilly, one of Howard's clients whose case was about to be called, and Howard had not yet appeared in the courtroom. Almost everyone regularly practicing law in this court was aware of Howard's customary tendency to be late for court, but he had outdone himself this time. I asked others, but no one knew where he was. Sure enough, O'Reilly's case was the next one called. When O'Reilly walked up and stood before the judge by himself, Laura Berg quickly moved beside him and asked the O'Reilly case to be footed. This was not what Judge Armstrong wanted to hear, but the two in front of him were not the subject of his wrath, and he agreed to foot the case.

Barry Gibbons was one of the two other clients I had on the day's schedule, and I'd not been able to find him. When a young man entered the room, appearing to look around for somebody, I approached him and asked who he was. Luckily, it was Mr. Gibbons. We had only talked for a few seconds when his case was called. He and I walked up and stood in front of the judge and, like others before me, I asked the case to be footed so we could get ready. But the judge wasn't having it. Court had been in session for forty-five minutes and Judge Armstrong had concluded, not unfairly, that my client and I had just met, and he went after him.

"Mr. Gibbons, you were told at your arraignment you were required to meet with your attorney prior to this date and you were to be here by ten. When did you and Mr. Cole first meet?"

Ouch! It looked like, with Howard still not having arrived to take the beating, the judge was going to make this case the theatrical highlight of the morning.

Feeling Barry still had some protections from the Fifth and Sixth Amendments, I ask that I be given an opportunity to confer with my client before he responded to the court. Judge Armstrong did agree to foot the case but warned that we had better be prepared to answer his question when the case was called again. Barry and I quickly retreated into the public seating.

My other client, Dave Walters, still had not appeared. When his case was called, I stepped forward and admitted Mr. Walters was not present and asked the case to be continued a week. Denying my request, the judge issued a bench warrant and set the bail at $10,000. Walter was only charged with possession of a stolen credit card, and he had no prior felony convictions. His failure to appear probably meant that when he did appear in court, he'd be in custody and would lose his opportunity to contest the charges. He'd be offered a plea deal that meant serving less time in jail than the amount of time he'd wait to get his case to trial.

Judge Armstrong continued to call through the list of defendants, followed by all the cases that had been footed. When he came again to the O'Reilly case, Howard had still not appeared. Laura stepped in again and O'Reilly's case was continued a week.

"Ms. Berg," said the judge. "Tell Mr. Graham that he is to call and schedule a time to meet me in chambers and bring his checkbook."

Jack Gardner, the prosecutor in my trial with Cindy, was handling the Gibbons case. While the court was dealing with other cases, he and I had conferred, and we had an agreed order ready. I instructed Gibbons he was not to utter a word when the case was called again. I would tell the judge he was exercising his Fifth Amendment Right to remain silent and assure the court the case was on schedule for resolution within the legal time limit. When the case got called again, it was towards the end of the calendar and the courtroom was beginning to clear. With the audience of other defendants almost gone, Judge Armstrong gave me a raised eyebrow, signaling he knew this was the case on which he had promised further interrogation, but he signed the agreed order without further discussion.

As I walked out of the courtroom, I passed Howard just coming in, still tying his tie. He had been over at the jail and had forgotten about the O'Reilly case until Laura called him on his cell phone. When he finished tying his tie, he walked into the courtroom. I did not want to miss the highlight of the day, so I turned and followed him in and stood alongside several other public defenders to watch the show.

Judge Armstrong saw Howard the moment he walked in the door, but continued to deal with the cases until they were done.

"Mr. Graham, thanks for coming. We are done with the calendar. Come back into chambers where we can talk."

Disappointed we weren't going to get to see the show, the rest of us walked back to the office. On the way, we were guessing what was going to happen to Howard, and whining about prosecutors, judges, and our clients, and about the flood of new cases that had been assigned to us.

—

I had several matters to handle in court that afternoon, which needed a little more preparation, so I turned down the invitation to go out to lunch and instead wolfed down the sandwich I had brought from home while I reviewed the paperwork I needed for court. As time for court approached, I headed back to the courthouse. On the way, I met Howard and learned Judge Armstrong had let him off again. I guess the skills of a used car salesman are as important to being a good public defender as being on time to court.

First up for me in the afternoon was the Gilbert Martin case. We had him scheduled to plead guilty to the reduced charge of theft in the third degree and then get sentenced. Because the value of the goods he'd taken from the Safeway was small, it was going to be a gross misdemeanor, not a felony, and the prosecutor Janet Coleman and I were going to agree to a 30-day sentence which would have Gilbert out of jail in another week if he had eared all his good-time, two weeks if he hadn't. I'd been up to see Gilbert in the jail, and we'd gone over the several pages of the guilty-plea statement we'd be submitting to the judge. Our discussion went slowly, and Gilbert kept looking away and had to be brought back into our conversation. However, I was satisfied he understood what the paperwork said. He was obviously mentally ill, but definitely not without a reasonable intelligence.

Gilbert had been brought from jail to the courtroom and when his case was called, he and I 'approached the bench.' I handed the guilty-plea statement to Colman, who checked a few things and handed it, via the court clerk, to the judge. Judge Armstrong was again on the bench and Colman told him, in the interest of justice, she was reducing the charge. I told the judge I had gone over all the terms of the statement with Gilbert and was satisfied he fully understood them all and was knowingly and intelligently entering a plea of guilty to the charge of third-degree theft.

Gilbert was shaking with nervousness as the judge began his inquiry. It had to be terribly difficult for him to control those thoughts that constituted his mental illness in order to rationally dialogue with this "center of power" seated well above him in a matter so important. At first, Gilbert didn't answer the judge, but with some encouragement from me, he was eventually able to tell the judge we had reviewed the statement and he understood what it said.

Seeing the difficulty Gilbert was having, the judge cut to the issue he thought was most critical. "Mr. Martin, what is the sentence the prosecutor going to recommend?"

"Thirty days, with credit for time served."

"Do you understand I don't have to follow that recommendation and can sentence you to anything up to 364 days?"

"Yes, I know that. Can you let me out today?"

"Yes, I could do that, but do you also know I could decide to have you serve all 364 days?"

"Yes."

With that, Armstrong accepted the plea, and I took a little sigh of relief. Everybody in the room, including the judge, could see Gilbert had mental problems, and the court's usual response in such circumstances is to order a competency evaluation. Taking the time to get professional assurance Gilbert was competent to enter this guilty plea might have provided the criminal justice system a greater claim to virtue, but would have come at considerable expense for Gilbert, more time spent in jail and a greater disruption of the treatment he needed.

Turning now to the sentencing, as promised, Coleman recommended a 30-day sentence with credit for time served. I had already submitted our social work report that had been prepared by Meredith, showing she had re-connected Gilbert with his mental health services and had arranged for some services for Gilbert's mother to help make things go more smoothly at home.

The judge was on board.

"Mr. Martin, I am going to follow the agreed recommendation and sentence you to 364 days in jail, but suspend 334 days, leaving you with 30 days to serve with credit for time you have already served."

In a good world, Gilbert would stay in treatment and get greater control of himself. In our world, people like Gilbert will often keep having lapses and keep coming back into a criminal justice system totally incapable of dealing with them.

—

Ray Langus' case was also on for a plea and sentencing. Since we had only been able to schedule the case that morning, there was a lot of scrambling to get the plea statement and the sentencing paperwork ready. I had handed Ray the plea statement on my way to do Gilbert's case so he could preview it, but I hadn't discussed it with him. As we were called before the court, Ray told me he had done this before and knew what he was doing and didn't want any delay that would keep him off the next bus back to prison. In front of the judge, Ray did all—well almost all—the talking, and he handled it perfectly. His plea was accepted, and he got the agreed sentence. As the law required, the time on new sentence ran concurrent with the sentence he was already serving, and he even got Judge Armstrong give him credit on the new sentence from the day he'd begun to serve the other sentence, which left him with only four additional months to serve. Ray did not have any good cards, but he played to his best advantage what he had.

—

We had prepared well for Jeff's bail hearing. Polly had made calls to his brother, who had agreed to have Jeff stay with him, and to the employer, where Jeff was scheduled to start work, to ensure there would be a job for him there. I had called Jeff's wife Darlene, who completely supported Jeff being out of custody. We had filed a brief with this information, with copies sent directly to the judge and to the prosecutor assigned to Jeff's case, Bob Winston. Winston's only commitment to me before court had been that his office would "think about it."

Jeff and I stepped in front of the judge when his case was called. I asked for Jeff's release on his personal recognizance. I made reference to the information we had provided in the brief and argued allowing Jeff to be released to take the quality employment waiting for him would enable him to provide for his wife and two children. I acknowledged he had some significant prior convictions but argued his last offense was committed thirteen years ago, and he had been out of custody, building his life crime free for nine years.

Winston had a surprise for us all. He had just received information from Missouri that Jeff's 1998 conviction was a first-degree burglary, not a second-degree burglary as we had been led to believe. He told the judge that made the current charge a "third strike" and asked that bail be set at million dollars because of the high risk of flight.

I felt frozen where I stood. Jeff was pulling on my arm, wanting to know what this was all about. Everyone in the room knew something big had happened. Seeing Jeff's emotional level rising, the guards escorting him moved closer. Judge Armstrong set the bail at $200,000, and Jeff was quickly taken to a private interview room so he and I could talk.

"Jeff, your case is now a three-strikes case. Under Washington law, when a person gets convicted on separate occasions of crimes listed as 'most serious offenses,' upon conviction for the third such offense, the sentence will automatically be life in prison without any possibility for release. We always knew your vehicular homicides counted as one strike and your current charge of second-degree assault would also be a strike if you were convicted. What we did not know until just now was one of those Missouri burglaries was a first-degree burglary, which is a most serious offense. If you do get convicted of the assault charge, it would be your third strike."

Jeff was outraged.

"Life in prison, that's ridiculous, I didn't hurt Darlene."

I told him I was shocked too, but we were going to use every resource possible to avoid that third strike. I don't think that calmed his outrage because it didn't do anything to my state of anxiety. I was feeling a great sense of urgency to get in touch with Maureen Miller, the assigned investigator for the case and get going on our interviews with Darlene and the other witnesses, to plan my approach to the prosecutor about a plea deal, and to get all advice possible from the other lawyers. There wasn't much more either Jeff or I wanted to say right then. On my signal, the guards came to take him back to jail, and I went back to the office.

CHAPTER FOUR
Lori Lucas

Joyce Benson and I were classmates at the University of Washington Law School. While I was doing my internship at a public defender office, Joyce was doing one at a prosecutor's office. We opposed each other on a couple of cases during that time, but none of them went to trial. Thinking she was on a good path for herself, I was surprised to see she had applied for the same job I did at HCPD. When I got the job, she sent me a nice card of congratulations, but I could see she was disappointed. When an unexpected opening came up, I gave her a call. She was about to take a job with the Skagit County Prosecutor but applied with us instead and we have been colleagues here for five years. We have often talked about the career choices we made. There is a lot of slander against prosecutors thrown around at HCPD: They lie, they are lazy, and they're just plain blind to the interest of justice. Joyce complains as adamantly as any of us, but she often takes the opportunity to defend the prosecutors for their honorable work in a cause we had to appreciate. There is one other thing that set Joyce apart from the rest of the public defenders, maybe because of her close encounter with the other side of the law. While many of us started dressing more informally in court when not in front of a jury, Joyce was always dressed-to-impress whenever she was in court, regardless of the occasion.

I shared with Joyce my frustrations about the Harris case. She shared with me a trial she did where her client wasn't facing as big a blow as Jeff was, but the consequences her client faced were still quite extreme.

Lori Lucas had been charged with first-degree criminal mistreatment. Her infant daughter Anne had poked a stick in her own eye. Although the child had obviously suffered a serious injury, Lori did not take her to the doctor. A neighbor, Kim Harper, had stopped in several days after the accident and, upon seeing the injury, called 911. At the hospital, it was determined the delay in seeking treatment had cost Anne her vision in that eye. When the authorities learned what had happened, Lori was charged and taken to jail, and Child Protective Services took custody of Anne.

At the time of the incident, Lori and Anne were living at the home of an older man, Mark Simmons. She was keeping house in exchange for room and board. To divert any suspicion from him of criminal involvement, Simmons' lawyer had presented a letter to the police stating he was not the father of the child and had assumed no responsibility for her care.

Lori was 22. She had run away from her parents' home in rural South Dakota about the time she got pregnant with Anne. She and her boyfriend moved to his home in the state of Washington, but she got dumped when she refused to get an abortion. She got help through her pregnancy at the local mission and after Anne was born, she got the job of live-in maid with Mr. Simmons.

When Joyce first met Lori in the jail, everything in Lori's life had gone wrong. She was feeling terribly guilty about what happened to her daughter and was a physical mess. Her long hair was unkempt, and she was shaking and cried often. She had arrived at the jail with nothing but the clothes she was wearing.

Simmons had told the police when they arrested Lori that she was not to come back and that she needed to get her things right away or they would be thrown out and by that time, as far as Lori knew, her things were gone. What had her most upset, of course, was that authorities had taken her child away. She had wanted to just plead guilty to get this business over with so she could focus on getting Anne back. However, she was facing five years in prison and a guilty verdict would likely result in a permanent loss of her daughter.

Lori's legal problems were substantial, but more immediate where her personal problems, so Joyce's first task was to get help from one of our social workers. David Philips was assigned to the case. He'd come to work at HCPD after a career in the Army where he lost a leg to a roadside bomb while serving in Afghanistan. During his recoupment, he obtained a master's degree in social work. It was a little difficult for him at first, working on behalf of law breakers, but it didn't take him long to see our clients were real people too often needing the kind of help he was trained to give, rather than the condemnation most people show for them.

Upon receiving the assignment, David went right over to the jail to talk to Lori. The next day he was in Joyce's office with a long list of things that needed to be done, but with some serious doubts as to whether Lori had the strength to face the difficulties involved. Even if the prospects were a little dim, Joyce and David decided to put together a plan.

First on the list was a place for Lori to stay if the court could be convinced to release her from jail. There were two problems with that: the number of shelter beds available in Hudson County was far below the need. And, while it is standard for the court to insist a defendant have a place to live before letting them out of jail, because of the limited number of beds, organizations that provided them didn't allow someone to reserve a bed while still in custody. Joyce was going to propose that the release order give David the responsibility for finding a place for Lori to stay and monitor her whereabouts between release and trial. On rare occasions in the past, the courts had agreed to this, but it always left the social worker in a potentially difficult position. As part of the defense team, David operates under the same requirement of confidentiality lawyers have. Yet under the agreement Joyce was proposing, he would be compelled to turn Lori in if she failed to comply with the terms.

Once out, Lori was going to need a job. She was going to have to find that on her own, but David was going to put her in touch with a couple of organizations that would help. It turned out Lori was less than a year from her high school diploma and always dreamed of going to college, so a source for training for the high school equivalency examination was also on the list. David had resources available for that as well. The next step was to see what the court was going to say.

Joyce scheduled a bail hearing in the video court. Her efforts to convince the prosecutor assigned to Lori's case, Jean Livingston, to agree to a release were unsuccessful, so it was going to be up to Joyce and Lori to convince the judge to accept the plan. Joyce scheduled the hearing for a day Judge Armstrong would be presiding. Some of her colleagues thought that was a bad idea because Armstrong was well known at HCPD to be a tough judge. Joyce decided to go with him because he was also equally hard on the prosecutors and his decision would be independent of the political correctness prosecutors like to rely on.

The day came for the hearing. David's work with Lori, over the several days it took to get ready for the hearing, helped her to develop some level of confidence that it wasn't the end of the world and there was a shot at this. Lori had also been talking to the lawyer representing her in her efforts to regain custody of Anne, and they had obtained appointment of a psychologist with expertise in parenting to, hopefully, prepare a favorable report. She arrived in court, this time more relaxed than at her last hearing and with her hair carefully combed. When her case was called, Lori and Joyce took their seats in front of the video camera and the television screen showing the prosecutor and judge.

"Your Honor," began Joyce, "we are asking the court to release Ms. Lucas on her personal recognizance. She has no criminal convictions and no history of failing to appear in court."

"Ms. Benson," said Judge Armstrong. "I read your brief and I see you don't have a place for your client to live."

"That's right, Your Honor, but as outlined in the brief, our social worker David Philips is prepared to work with Ms. Lucas to find and maintain housing. There is emergency housing available and once out of jail other, more long-term shelters can be found."

"Judge," responded Livingston. "We object to a release. A young child was permanently injured in this incident and the defendant is charged with a Class B felony and is looking at five years in prison. Ms. Lucas comes from South Dakota and has no close friends or family here in Washington. The court needs to keep close track of the defendant so we can deal with this terrible crime."

"Your Honor," said Joyce, "This was a terribly unfortunate incident. However, it is going to be up to a jury to decide if there is a crime here. The crime charged is a crime of negligence. Nobody is saying Ms. Lucas committed an intentional harm. And she does have a close family member in this community providing all the motivation needed for her to appear for all her court hearings— her daughter Anne. Ms. Lucas has a lawyer and is actively involved in the court proceedings involving the custody of the child. The court's interests here include protecting the community and the facts here leave nothing to suggest Ms. Lucas presents a danger to anyone. The court also has an interest in having Ms. Lucas appear for court, but in serving that interest the court can't discriminate against her because of her lack of resources. Your Honor, we are offering the court a plan that will accommodate all the court's interests."

At that point, Lori spoke up. "Sir, all I want is to be able to deal with these charges and get my daughter back. I am going to be coming to court until I get all that done."

After a couple of moments of silence, Judge Armstrong addressed himself to Lori.

"Ms. Lucas, I am going to take a chance, and I am thinking it might be a pretty risky chance. I am going to order your release. You are going to have to work with Mr. Philips to find a place where you can stay and keep in touch with him until this case is finished."

What a good piece of luck! With the judge's ruling in play, Joyce escorted Lori back to her seat, handed her David's card with instructions to call when she was released, then walked quickly back to the office to talk to David about his next step. He had arranged for an emergency shelter that would only last four days, leaving him on a tight schedule to get the rest of the necessities in place. David thought it would be good to get Lori's parents involved. Lori had made no effort to contact them since running away with her boyfriend, Anne's reluctant father. Lori didn't think they knew about her pregnancy, let alone that they had become grandparents. Lori didn't remember her parents' phone number, but it took David only five minutes to find it on the internet. When contacted, the Lucases were relieved to learn their daughter was ok. When she had run away without leaving any message, they had concluded she didn't want to have anything more to do with them. They were more than happy to reestablish communication. They'd thought she might be pregnant and were happy she had a daughter and they a granddaughter. But, of course, they were saddened by the child's loss of an eye and all the legal troubles for their daughter. At that time, they didn't have the funds or the time away from the work on their farm to come to Washington.

The focus from here on was going to be on the legal side of the case. Looking at the facts more closely, it appeared Anne was playing by herself on the floor while Lori was cleaning the kitchen and Simmons was watching television. She had picked up a stick the dog had brought in. Waving it in the air uncontrollably as babies do, she poked herself in the eye. Blood flowed from around the eye and in short order the eye turned red. Lori had cleaned away the blood, which soon stopped flowing and put cold compresses in the eye until Anne stopped crying.

Tony Hawkins was assigned as Lori's investigator. Tony is the most senior investigator at HCPD and is always telling everyone, with some justification, that he has "seen everything." When he first got the assignment, he told Joyce she didn't have a chance, but after reading the police reports, he found a couple of angles he thought could be investigated. He and Joyce decided they would have some heavy interviews with Simmons, Harper the neighbor, and the treating physician, Dr. Heather Allen. They would also look at hiring an expert witness to deal with the medical factors.

—

On the day before Lori's Omnibus hearing, David walked into Joyce's office to announce he had lost her. She had remained at the emergency shelter for the full four days and then left with others without calling him. David hadn't been able to get more permanent housing, but Lori should have stayed in touch. The next day, Joyce went to the Omnibus hearing, pretty sure Lori had taken the easy path and just run away. When she arrived in the courtroom, she looked around the public seating and, sure enough, Lori was not there. Livingston was not offering to agree to a guilty plea to a reduced charge, so the lawyers had agreed to ask the court to just confirm the case for trial. Of course, with Lori not showing up, that order was going to turn into an arrest warrant.

The judge had proceeded down the list of cases and was

within two of Lori's case when Joyce got a tap on the shoulder. Turning around, to her great relief, she saw Lori. Her clothes were dirty, but her face was clean, and her hair was nicely combed. Being there allowed Lori to avoid a warrant. The court hearing she was required to attend lasted only twenty seconds, during which nothing was said, and the judge just signed off on the order that had been prepared by the lawyers.

Joyce called David on her cellphone. He said he'd meet them back at the office, so when Joyce's other case was done, she and Lori walked to the office together. On the way, Lori explained that when she had to leave the emergency shelter, she'd hooked up some others who were also leaving, and they had all gone to a homeless camp down by the river where she had spent three nights, without access to a working cellphone, waiting for this day in court. When they got to the office, David told Lori she might have to spend a night or two more at the camp, but she was nearing the top of the waiting list at a shelter where she could stay until trial and could continue trying to find a job and some arrangements for schooling.

As the trial date approached, the biggest task was the investigation. Tony and Joyce had an easy conversation with Ms. Harper. She was glad to be able to intervene but was sad she hadn't paid her visit to the Simmons house in time to save Anne's eye. She had seen Lori and Anne out in the yard but was a little surprised to learn Lori was there as a live-in housekeeper. It had been a little difficult to schedule a time with Dr. Allen. When finally arranged, Allen explained it was her professional opinion that, with timely intervention, Anne's eyesight could have been saved. Tony thought that opinion could be open to challenge, but the two doctors he contacted for a second opinion had both advised him their opinions would be the same as Dr. Allen's. The interview with Mr. Simmons was a much bigger struggle. He was, of course, accompanied by two of his lawyers and he had been well trained to say he had no responsibility for the care of Anne and that he had suggested they call 911 when the accident occurred. Joyce spent many hours, some late at night, putting together her cross-examination of these witnesses and preparing Lori for her testimony.

The trial date arrived. The case had been assigned to Judge Armstrong's court and when he saw Lori was appearing out of custody on her own, he took a moment to thank her for confirming his judgment to release her.

The first order of business was "motions in limine." These were issues the Judge needed to resolve before the testimony began because the judge's rulings on the motions would affect what evidence the two sides could present. One motion was absolutely critical to Joyce's case, and it had to do with the testimony of Dr. Allen.

"Your Honor, I move that Dr. Allen be prohibited from offering an opinion as to whether the failure to get prompt aid for Anne constituted criminal negligence."

"I certainly object to that, Your Honor," said Livingston. "It is Dr. Allen's expert opinion, one which the defense has had plenty of time to study, that treatment provided right after the accident would have saved the child's eyesight."

"Your Honor, we are prepared for the doctor to offer that opinion. However, criminal negligence is a legal standard and involves a lot more than what is contained in the doctor's opinion. That is the question for the jury."

Joyce had to win this motion. No jury would have disagreed with an opinion from the doctor. Judge Armstrong looked out in silence and after several moments, "I am going to reserve ruling on this motion because I need to do some research. For now, Ms. Livingston, you will not suggest that Dr. Allen has such an opinion, and you, Ms. Benson, will not suggest that she doesn't." Joyce wasn't happy to have this critical issue left in the air, but at least she hadn't lost.

When other pretrial matters had been resolved, the jury panel, those 30 people from whom 12 would be selected to try the case, were brought into the courtroom and jury selection got underway.

The obvious objective of Livingston's selections was to get jurors from the middle class and up who never had to worry about the cost of getting medical aid when it was needed. Joyce's objective, probably equally obvious to Livingston, was to get jurors with some appreciation of the hard times for people without resources. The jury selected ended up as a mixture of both.

Opening statements were the last order of business for the day. Livingston's case was straight forward. As the child's parent, Lori had a special responsibility to provide needed medical attention, and she had failed to provide it by not taking the child to the hospital in time to save her eyesight. Most of what Joyce needed to say involved the subtilties of criminal negligence which needed to be saved for closing argument, so Joyce spent her opening introducing Lori and the circumstances leading her into single parenthood two thousand miles from home and working as a live-in housekeeper.

CHAPTER FIVE

It All Came Down to This

Testimony began first thing the next day. There was nothing controversial in the testimony of the first two witnesses, one of the emergency responders who took Anne to the hospital and the police officers who arrested Lori. The third witness was the neighbor, Kim Harper. Her testimony on direct examination was straight forward. Armed with information revealed in Tony's investigation, on cross-examination Joyce got her to describe for the jury her greater than ordinary medical knowledge, the five years she had spent as an emergency room nurse before retiring to become a receptionist for a doctor in general practice. In her time at the hospital, she hadn't seen an injury like Anne's but had been trained about the particular danger of puncture wounds around the eye.

Dr. Allen was going to be the next witness, but as she approached the witness stand, Judge Armstrong called the morning recess, and the jury went back into the jury room.

"Dr. Allen, I want you and our two lawyers who will be asking you questions to listen to my ruling. Doctor, you are going to be asked if you have an opinion based on your professional training and experience whether the child's eyesight could have been saved if she had been brought to the hospital right after the injury occurred. You can answer that question and explain why you think so. However, you cannot say that it was wrong or negligent for that not to have been done.

"Ms. Livingston, you can ask all the questions you want regarding procedures that could have saved the girl's eyesight if she had been seen immediately, but you may not ask the doctor whether the failure to obtain immediate attention was negligence. That is for the jury to decide and for you to argue in your closing.

"Ms. Benson, you can't suggest in any question on cross-examination, or argue in closing, that Dr. Allen doesn't have an opinion as to whether your client was negligent."

The judge's ruling was all Joyce could have hoped for. She knew any effort on her part to get Dr. Allen to say the delay was not negligence would have failed badly.

It was a short recess, and the jury was soon back in the courtroom. Dr. Allen took the witness stand, and the trial was again underway. In her testimony, the doctor described how Anne's eyeball had been penetrated by the stick from the side. There had been a surgical procedure that could have repaired that, but the delay in getting the child to the hospital had caused the damage to become unrepairable. From talking to Tony, Joyce knew Dr. Allen's opinion would hold up and any effort on her part to attack it would only make it look stronger to the jury. However, Joyce did have a couple of questions.

"Did you have an opportunity to look at the general condition of the child?"

"Yes, in preparation for the surgery, she was given a complete physical, and she was otherwise completely healthy and was an appropriate weight and height for a child of her age."

"Where did the stick enter the eye?

"It was the left eye, and the penetration came from the left side of the child's face."

"Was the puncture visible in the normally visible part of the eye?"

"You could certainly see blood in the eyeball and coming around the eye, but the puncture itself was over to the left."

That was as far as Joyce wanted to go on cross-examination.

On her re-direct Livingston asked, "How long in the course of your initial examination did it take you to detect the puncture wound."

"Well, I knew just looking at the eye there was a puncture, and I could see it directly just by gently pushing on the skin."

You could see the doctor had made a big impression on the jury.

Livingston had one more witness, Mr. Simmons, and he walked into the courtroom accompanied by his lawyer, Jason Brampton. Realizing there might be an issue to resolve, Judge Armstrong declared another short break. With the jurors out of the room, Brampton stepped forward.

"Your Honor, Ms. Lucas was employed by Mr. Simmons and living in his house at the time of this incident and Mr. Simmons was present, watching TV when it happened. Although Mr. Simmons never did, as the statute says. 'assume the responsibility to provide' to the child 'the basic necessities of life' his testimony could support that kind of claim and if not as a principal, as an accomplice."

Livingston spoke up. "Your Honor, we have already told Mr. Brampton we have no intention of charging his client with a crime in this matter."

"We knew that Your Honor," said Brampton, "but we don't think there should even be any accusations made in this trial that could affect Mr. Simmons' reputation.

It was Joyce's turn. "Your Honor, it wouldn't be right for the court to foreclose us from making any kind of accusation supported by evidence that could be used in our defense."

"Ms. Benson is right," responded the judge. "I am not going

to make any ruling foreclosing any questions or argument at this point.

"Having said that, Mr. Brampton, I want to be sure we are all playing by the rules here. You are here representing a witness, not a party, so unless I address you with a question.... or an order, you need to remain silent while your client is testifying before this jury. I assume you have thoroughly briefed your client on his testimony. However, if Mr. Simmons needs to ask you a question, he can so signal by saying 'I have a question,' and we will remove the jury and deal with his question."

Simmons finally got on the stand and testified. He told the jury he had hired Lori through a site on the internet about ten months ago. In exchange for room and board and some cash for necessities for her and her daughter, she prepared meals and kept house. On the evening of the accident, Simmons testified he was watching television when he heard Anne scream. He went to see what had happened and found Lori holding Anne with blood flowing from the child's face. He suggested, in his words, that "she might want to call 911." Lori had cleaned up the blood and applied a cold compress. Over the next two days, the child was whiney. When Mrs. Harper came over and got a look at the child, 911 was called and an ambulance took the child and Lori to the hospital. As carefully scripted for him by his lawyer, Simmons mentioned several times he took no responsibility in trying to deal with Anne's injury. Livingston completed her examination, and it was time for Joyce's cross-examination.

"Mr. Simmons, how old are you?"

"51."

"Do you know how old Ms. Lucas is?"

"Not exactly, I think she is about 25."

"Did you closely examine Anne's eye after the accident?"

"No, I left that to Ms. Lucas."

"Did you have any discussions with Ms. Lucas about the

condition of her daughter after that one suggestion that she might call 911."

"No."

"Do you have a car?"

"Of course."

"Does Ms. Lucas have a car?"

"No."

"Do you know where the hospital is?"

"Yes."

"Would it be fair to say that the hospital is less than 10 miles from your house?"

"I think that is probably correct."

"Did you ever offer or suggest that you would take the child to the hospital?"

"No, but she never asked."

With that, Joyce's cross examination was complete. Livingston had no further questions for Simmons and no further witnesses, and it was time for the defense case. Tony was listed as a potential witness in case any of the prosecutor's witnesses strayed from what they had said during their interviews, but that didn't happen. Lori was going to be the only defense witness. Her testimony was going to be simple and straight forward, and she had been as well prepared as possible for Livingston's cross-examination. That young woman Joyce met at the arraignment would have failed miserably, but the one about to take the stand had a real chance.

Joyce began by asking Lori to tell her story, running away from home with a boyfriend, being dumped by the boyfriend for refusing to get an abortion, giving birth to Anne, and finding a job and place to live with Mr. Simmons. It was hard for her to talk about the night of her daughter's injury. Upon hearing Anne scream, she ran to her child, wiped the blood from her face, and held her tight. When she got a close look, there was blood coming from around the eye. There was no damage to the eyeball that she could see, but later it did turn red.

"Ms. Lucas, why didn't you take Anne to the hospital?"

"I didn't know what to do. Mr. Simmons walked over, but he didn't seem too worried. He said I could call 911 if I wanted to, but I knew that would cost a lot of money, and I didn't have any money or insurance. Anne calmed down after a while and I just thought things were going to be OK."

"Did you know you could have gotten emergency medical help even without insurance or a payment plan?"

"Yes, but my parents spent years struggling to pay some hospital bills, and I knew eventually I could have a huge bill to pay."

"Lori, do you know now you made a mistake and, as a result of that mistake, your daughter Anne has lost the vision in her left eye?"

Starting to cry Lori answered: "Yes."

With that Joyce decided she and Lori had covered all the bases, and it was now Livingston's turn to conduct her cross-examination.

"Ms. Lucas, would you take your car in to be seen by a mechanic if it wasn't running right?"

"I don't have a car."

"If you did have a car and it wasn't working right?"

"I might look under the hood and see if it was something I could fix like a loose wire, but I would take it in to a mechanic if I had enough money to pay for the repair."

"Do you have any training in medical science?"

"No."

"Would you agree that it if you had something medically wrong, it would be better to get help from people who knew what they were doing than to trust your own judgement?"

"If it was serious enough, yes."

"And this poke in your daughter's eye was serious enough that you should have gotten the expert help that would have saved her eyesight?"

"Yes, Ms. Livingston. I will admit I made a terrible mistake, and I am never going to forgive myself for having made it. But I made that mistake because I didn't know what Dr. Allen knows."

Livingston was done, and Lori had handled her questions as well as anyone could have. The defense rested and closing arguments were next.

The judge took a break, and Lori and Joyce decided to relax for a few moments in an attorney conference room. Lori began telling Joyce about her efforts to regain custody of Anne. The psychologist her other lawyer had hired had given Lori several psychological tests and conducted several long interviews with her, and the preliminary results were positive. She went on to tell Joyce about her part-time job where her boss had promised a full-time employment, with benefits within a couple of months.

Lori had also been studying and was scheduled to take her high school equivalency test in two weeks. As Lori spoke and Joyce listened, they were both feeling the weight of the trial on that future.

With the court back in session, Judge Armstrong began by reading his instructions to the jury explaining the law they were to apply: "A parent of a child commits first degree criminal mistreatment if with criminal negligence he or she causes great bodily harm to the child by withholding any of the necessities of life.

"A person is criminally negligent when he or she fails to be aware of a substantial risk that a wrongful act may occur, and that failure constitutes a gross deviation from the standard of care that a reasonable person would use in the same situation."

Livingston's closing argument went straight to the elements of the crime charged. As the parent of the child, the defendant had a special obligation of care for the child by providing the basic necessities of life, including medical treatment. The defendant acted with criminal negligence, causing great bodily harm to the child when she failed to take the child to the hospital for treatment, resulting in the loss of vision in the injured eye. Because of this failure, the defendant was guilty of criminal mistreatment in the first degree.

As Joyce stood to present her closing argument, Lori grabbed her arm and motioned to the door where David entered in the company of a woman.

"That is my mother."

When Lori's parents had received the call from Lori that David had arranged—after almost three years of hearing nothing and then learning of the trouble she was in—they felt an urgent need to come to see her. Farm duties and the lack of money had hampered their efforts. But they finally managed to book a flight for Lori's mother. Her trip began with a long drive in the middle of the night from their home in White Owl, South Dakota to Rapid City, followed by a flight to Minneapolis, and from there, after a two-hour layover, a flight that brought her to Seattle on the second day of the trial. As prearranged, David met her at the airport and brought her directly to court.

Judge Armstrong was not going to tolerate any more delays, so Lori's mother was just going to have to wait to give her daughter a hug. Joyce stood and faced the jury.

"It is certainly true Lori Lucas' daughter Anne suffered great bodily harm in the loss of vision in her left eye. It is true that as Anne's mother, Lori, has a special responsibility to provide Anne with the necessities of life, which includes obtaining medical attention when needed. And it is true that it was a mistake, a terrible mistake, that will haunt Lori for the rest of her life, to have failed to have taken Anne to the hospital right when the injury occurred. However, what is not true is that Lori's mistake constituted an act of criminal negligence and that is because it was not a 'gross deviation from the standard of care that a reasonable person would exercise in the same situation.' Why it's not is what I want to talk to you about.

"What was Lori's 'situation?' She is a very young woman. Her parents were a thousand miles away; her child's father had run out of the picture; she did not have others in her generation with whom to communicate, but instead was living in a household with a much older man with whom she had little in common and who took no responsibility for helping out when this accident occurred. She had no place to turn outside her own best judgments in deciding how to respond. Lori's 'situation' also included the fact that she apparently had no transportation to the hospital unless she called for an ambulance and no health insurance to pay a medical bill, which then or later would be overwhelming.

"From within that 'situation,' Lori cleaned away the blood from around Anne's eye and applied a cold compress. She examined the eye but saw no puncture wound and without the expertise of Dr. Allen or even the medical experience of Ms. Harper and within the context of that 'situation' made what I would suggest was a reasonable choice of action. But, as what can happen from time to time in anybody's life, where a reasonable choice of action ends up being a wrong choice, Lori's decision was wrong.

"Members of the jury, even if you decide Lori had the tools to make a better decision, keep in mind that being wrong isn't criminal negligence. It must be a 'gross deviation' from what that reasonable person would have chosen to do, and that just didn't happen here. I ask you to bring back a verdict of not-guilty."

Livingston had the final word and tried to suggest that the standard of care was the same for everybody and suggested that the seriousness of what happened to Anne by itself proved criminal negligence. When she was done, the jury was sent to the jury room to deliberate on a verdict.

When the jury had left the room, the judge declared the court in recess. Lori walked to where her mother was standing and in a flood of tears, they hugged each other. There would be some time before the jury returned with a verdict, so Joyce, David, and Lori and her mother walked back to the office.

There, while David and Joyce prowled around the office looking for conversations to take their minds off the pending verdict, Lori and her mother—named Anne, as we should have guessed—went to a conference room to share the events of the last few years, here and in White Owl.

Joyce thought she had put the legal case together as well as it could have been done. However, a bigger part of the case was Lori's ability to get it together in the eight weeks between the arraignment and trial and to present herself so strongly in her testimony, including her responses to Livingston's cross-examination. The jury was going to have to take her seriously. That, of course, had most to do with the kind of character that had been there all along, but also was the result of the help David had given her in allowing that character to come out.

The custody of Anne was a question still in the hands of another court. But there could be no success there unless Lori won here first, and after about a two hour wait, the judge's law clerk called to say that the jury had a verdict. The four returned to the court and Joyce and Lori took their seats at counsel table. The jury entered; their verdict form was given to the judge who read it aloud.

"We, the jury, find the defendant Lori Lucas not guilty of the crime of criminal mistreatment in the first degree."

CHAPTER SIX

Walter Chandler

Sydney Johnson had been a lawyer at HCPD longer than anyone else and had experienced most of the stages of its history. A lot of the lawyers who worked here ended up leaving after a few years, some to practice in a private law office with the promise of better pay and fewer responsibilities and some just to get to work in the big city—Seattle. Sydney stayed against all those temptations. There are pictures from the early days at HCPD showing Sydney as the slender, well-dressed person he was, contrasting considerably from the larger, informally dressed version we see in the office these days.

He had recently finished a case, and I was interested to hear about it, knowing there is always something to learn from someone else. Sydney's client, Walter Chandler, had been charged with second-degree rape. He had agreed to give a ride home to a woman, Sandra Glenn, whom he had met at a bar. On the way, they stopped in a park and had sex in the back seat of Walter's car, after which he took her home to her apartment. Glenn's story was that Walter pulled into a dark parking lot in a city park and suggested they have sex. When she refused, he pulled her out of the car, push her into the back seat, threatened to hit her if she didn't stop resisting, and forced her to submit to vaginal and anal intercourse. When she got to her apartment, she called 911 and reported the incident to the police. The police had no trouble finding Walter later that night back at the same bar. The only fortunate thing for Walter was that he declined to offer the police his side of the story, allowing him to figure that out later. His first story to Sydney was that the woman was just lying. When tests came back showing Walter's DNA in fluids taken from her body, his story became that the woman was a prostitute and had consented to the sex but had gotten mad at him when he refused to pay extra for the addition of the anal sex.

With all his experience working with clients, Sydney was never able to get around the shields Walter was holding up. Walter had never been through anything like this before. He had been marched into the video court where he uttered the words "not guilty" on cue from the stranger sitting next to him—our assigned lawyer. A few weeks later, he was taken to another court where Sydney, now at least someone he knew, and a prosecutor talked with a judge about his case, saying some things he could hardly hear, and which made no sense to him. When Sydney came to talk to him in his coat and tie, they talked about things that didn't make any sense either, the "offender score" and the "standard range" for his sentence, and the fact that penetration with a finger constituted sexual intercourse in the eyes of the law. Sydney knew Walter's confusion was not the result of a lack of intelligence. It had to do more with the fact that he had been dragged out of his world to play a game in a world he didn't recognize—where the odds were greatly against him. The fact that he had a lawyer on his team didn't completely right the ship. As Sydney put it, what had happened to each of them since birth and the people they had lived with had given them different worlds to live in, which made it impossible for either to fully understand the other. Sydney could tell from what Walter was saying he had been talking with other guys in his jail unit. What they might have lacked in lawyer skills, they likely made up in their understanding of Walter's world. Somewhere out of this confusing maze, Walter was going to have to make some of the most important decisions in his life.

The prosecutor had only offered to recommend the low end of the standard range if Walter pled guilty as charged. Walter didn't have any felony convictions, although if Glenn had been aware of his driving record, she would probably have refused the ride. With his zero-offender score, he was looking at a minimum sentence to be set by the judge between 78 and 102 months in prison, but that would not have been the end of his sentence. A state panel called the Indeterminate Sentence Review Board could, and probably would, extend that time and would have control of him when released, at least potentially, for the rest of his life. When Walter was told of the prosecutor's plea offer—plead guilty as charged—he declined and demanded to go to trial, as he should have.

Sydney's first step was to have an investigator assigned to help him interview Glenn and the other witnesses, and maybe find anything that might confirm Glenn had, at some time, engaged in prostitution. Tony Hawkins was assigned as the investigator. When he contacted Glenn directly, she refused to be interviewed by him and Sydney alone. The prosecutor's office had to set up the interview. An interview was conducted, but, in addition to Tony and Sydney, the prosecutor assigned to the case Beth Wilkerson and their witness advocate, who had been assigned to handle Glenn, were also in attendance.

Sandra Glenn was well groomed and appropriately dressed, not at all what one would think of as a prostitute. In the interview, Glenn said she was a student at the local college. She and several of her student friends had gone to the bar to celebrate the end of the term. Glenn decided she'd had enough to drink and wanted to leave early, and accepted Walter's offer for a ride. The sex was definitely not consensual, and she had physically resisted until Walter overpowered her and forced her into the back seat, at which point she stopped resisting. Walter had pulled off her clothes and force her to have vaginal and anal sex.

It was clear to both Tony and Sydney that Glenn was going to be a good witness for the prosecutor. She was quite clear about what happened down to the details. The blood test at the hospital when she went in for the rape exam did not show an alcohol level that might have allowed her to consent to something she later regretted. They still needed to investigate the prostitution angle and talk to the other women with her at the bar to see how innocent their get-together was.

Sydney's next step was another conversation with the prosecutor to try to get them down from their original plea offer, to see if there wasn't some version of third-degree rape that would satisfy them. For some time, prosecutors' offices across the country have had special assault units created to undo the previous history of official neglect of sex and domestic violence offenses against women. Wilkerson was the head of the county prosecutor's Special Assault Unit. She was one of the good prosecutors to deal with. Unlike many of her brethren, she answered email and phone messages promptly and a meeting was quickly arranged.

"Beth, we have the Chandler case coming up, and I want to see if we can get a better deal than plea as charged. This would be his first felony, and he was pretty intoxicated at the time and thought this was going to be a consensual thing. And he took her home afterwards."

"Well, I will give you part of that; this is his first felony, but considering what happened here, I am not going to buy the idea that he had any reason to think this was consensual. Even though you went past our last deadline, and we had to drag Sandra in for your interrogation, I will agree to continue to recommend the low end of the sentencing range for second-degree rape."

"I would like you to consider reducing the charge to third

degree rape and we could add one or two counts of assault in the third degree to raise the score."

"So, what is that—13 to 17 months? No way."

"Three counts of the assault?"

"No, that's only 15 to 20 months."

After looking through her file for a couple of minutes, Wilkerson offered: "I would consider doing rape three and three counts of assault three, all with sexual motivation. With sexual motivation attached, those assaults would count three points each and your guy would get 60 months. I am not promising that yet; I will have to consult with Ms. Glenn, and your guy is going to have to agree to it before I ask her."

That was about as well as Sydney thought he could do. The plea would knock his sentence down by at least a third. Next stop was the jail to talk with Walter. On his way back to the office, Sydney called Polly—he was her legal assistant too—and asked her to schedule him as soon as the jail had an opening and, luckily, there was an opening that afternoon.

Walter hadn't been brought down when Sydney arrived. Sydney was assigned to an interview room, went inside, and sat down to wait and think about how to handle the upcoming conversation. Wilkerson had all the evidence she needed. They had the DNA. Glenn's statements to the police on the night of the incident and at the defense interview were completely consistent. Tony had also had a chance to talk to the women Glenn was out with that night and confirmed that the purpose of the evening was nothing more than celebrating the end of the term. And he had found nothing to suggest Glenn or any of those women had been involved in prostitution. As big a hit as it was going to be for Walter, Sydney had concluded Wilkerson's plea offer was Walter's best option. It was important, however, for Sydney to present it in a way that, despite the communication barriers existing between the two of them, it didn't make Walter think he was being sold down the river. Sydney was the only one in this game on Walter's side, and Walter had to respect that when he made this terribly important decision.

Walter came in and took a seat and Sydney spent a few minutes telling him about the stages through which the trial would proceed, jury selection, opening statements, witness testimony, closing arguments and verdict. The judge couldn't make him testify and couldn't prevent him from testifying if he wanted to, but if he did testify, he would have to answer the prosecutor's questions whether he wanted to or not.

"Walter, the prosecutor has said she might be willing to let you plead to lesser charges, but if you agree to the deal, then Ms. Glenn is going to have to agree to it as well before it is a done deal. Here is the offer: You plead guilty to one count of rape in the third degree and three counts of assault in the third degree, each with a sexual motivation enhancement. That would give you an offender score of nine and a sentence of five years."

"Now you're talking about four crimes when before I was only charged with one."

"That's right, but the four crimes together give you a shorter time in prison than the 78 to 102 months you would get from the judge if you went to trial and lost. And you would avoid falling under the control by something called the Indeterminate Sentence Review Board. That Board has the power to extend the sentence set by the judge and keep you under state supervision, require you to undergo treatment and control what you did for the rest of your life."

Walter looked at Sydney.

"But I didn't rape that woman; the sex was consensual. I can name you a lot of women who would tell you they had had sex with me a number of times, and they always wanted it. I don't ever need to force sex on a woman. This Glenn woman is just lying."

Sydney asked Walter to think about it for a day and promised to come by the next morning to get his answer.

"I don't need a day. I can't do five years in prison, and she agreed to that sex."

With all the facts on the table, Sydney accepted Walter's decision and promised to come back the next day to talk about his testimony. The guard was called, Walter was led away, and Sydney went back to the office thinking they were probably headed down the wrong road. If Walter had gone to his doctor and requested a medication the doctor didn't think was right for him, the doctor would just refuse. A lawyer doesn't have that kind of authority and must accept the client's decision to "get the medicine" and go to trial.

Sydney did go to see Walter the first thing the next morning to get a clear picture of his version of what had happened that night. Before letting him speak, however, he made sure Walter was aware Tony had looked hard and found no evidence Glenn had ever engaged in prostitution.

"She's a college student intent on getting a degree, whose parents were helping her financially, and we had found no evidence she was an alcoholic or had been abusing drugs."

Walter then related that on the drive to her house, Glenn had touched him on his thigh and kissed him on the neck. One thing led to another, and he drove into a dark parking lot in a local park where they went into the back seat and had mutually active sex.

The story was clear; the trial was going to depend on whom the jury believed. Sydney reminded Walter he didn't have to testify, but there was nothing other than his testimony to present.

At the end of the session, Sydney told Walter he'd be back in the afternoon with another lawyer who would be asking him questions, playing the part of the prosecutor. Sydney brought Rachel Pierce to the visit with Walter that afternoon. Rachel had familiarized herself with the evidence in Walter's case and spent an hour-plus asking him the prosecutor's questions and grading his answers. Nobody is very good at being a witness without practice, particularly when their life is on the line. Walter was learning and not doing too badly by the end of our session.

—

The case was assigned out for trial in front of Judge Greenberg, and Sydney was in court first thing Monday morning, ready to go. The judge was holding a hearing from some divorce case. Considering the heated argument the two lawyers were having, Sydney was glad he was just trying a rape case. It wasn't long before the guards brought Walter into the courtroom dressed for trial. When the divorce hearing was completed, the two lawyers and the unhappy couple left the room, and the judge went back into his chambers to await the arrival of the jury. Walter was very nervous, as anyone would be facing a trial with this much riding on it. Sydney answered a couple of questions he had about procedure, followed by time when the two of them just sat there in silence. Wilkerson entered in the company of the lead detective and the two of them went to their desk and assembled paperwork.

After what seemed like a long wait, 30 jurors entered and sat down in the order of the numbers on their jury badges. The first thirteen sat in the jury box, as the presumptive jurors and alternate. The rest sat in the public seating. Sydney and Walter looked casually around the room at those from whom this jury would be taken, trying to anticipate how these people might respond to their case. With a different set of thoughts in her mind, Wilkerson viewed the same scene.

When everyone had situated themself, the law clerk called for the group to rise, declared Department Six of the Superior Court of the State of Washington in and for Hudson County to be in session with the Honorable Lawrence Greenberg presiding. With everyone on their feet, Judge Greenberg entered dressed in his black robe, took a position standing in front of the Washington and United States flags, and invited all to be seated. He told the jurors the name of the case and the criminal charge. He introduced Wilkerson and Sydney, who introduced Walter.

As Judge Greenberg began his inquiry of the panel, Walter handed Sydney the legal pad he'd been given for his notes with the words "plead guilty" written on it.

Sydney leaned over and Walter whispered. "I want to take the deal."

"But Walter, our deadline for taking the deal has long passed and there was no deal unless Ms. Glenn agreed to it."

"Can we ask?"

"I will try, but we are in the middle jury selection."

When the judge excused one of the jurors who had a vacation scheduled and paused to let her collect her things and leave the room, Sydney approached the bench and asked the judge to order a recess because he needed to discuss something with the prosecutor before things went any further. Judge Greenberg was not happy, something about "public defenders just fumbling around with the system when all these good citizens are taking time out of their lives to serve justice." He, nevertheless, agreed to a short break. While the judge explained things to the jurors, Sydney led Wilkerson out into the hall and told her: "My client wants to plead to the five-year deal. "

Wilkerson looked completely disgusted.

"I don't know why you guys can't get these things worked out before trial."

With both the judge and prosecutor thinking he was incompetent, Sydney knew full well why things like this don't always get worked out ahead of time. However, at that point, he didn't want to start an argument; he just needed Wilkerson's help.

"Would you please talk to Ms. Glenn?"

"I am making no promises. If it were just my decision we'd be going to trial, but the person I want to serve here is Sandra, your client's victim on December 11th who would again be your client's victim having to re-live it all again in public in front of a jury. But I will talk to her."

The two lawyers went back into the courtroom and approached the bench to fill in the judge on what had happened. Continuing in his frustration, Judge Greenberg decided to recess the proceedings and have the jury panel taken to the jury lounge, where there was plenty of room for them to relax while Wilkerson went to talk to Glenn. Walter and Sydney just sat and waited, with nothing to say to one another.

This sort of thing happens every now and again. To people without prior experience like Walter, a physical courtroom is going to feel like a strange place to be doing business. Add to that 30 people in the jury pool—almost all of whom were older than he and didn't look anything like the people he had been sharing his life with. It's not strange at all, for a defendant to have second thoughts about trial, or more likely, to have the second thoughts they'd been carrying with them take on priority. Sydney had always thought the plea was the best choice. Five years is a long time, but at the end of it, Walter would walk away—no probation, no treatment requirement, and no restrictions on where he could go or whom he could be with. Considering the various modifications of Walter's version of the facts, Sydney was quite sure the jury wasn't going to believe him.

Sydney and Walter had to wait quite a while, but eventually, Wilkerson did return and did offer Walter the deal—well almost. In addition to the rape in the third degree and three counts of assault in the third degree with sexual motivation, Walter would have to plead to an addition count of assault in the fourth degree with a six-month jail term, to be served prior to leaving for prison to then begin his five years. In addition, even though Glenn had been attending regular mental health therapy prior to the incident, restitution would be assessed for the cost of two years of counseling.

Walter wasn't happy with the additions, but realized there was no room for negotiations at that point and he agreed to the deal and the jurors were sent home. After Sydney discussed in detail the meaning of all seven pages of the guilty-plea document, Walter signed and initialed it as needed. Ready to go, Walter stood before the judge for entry of the guilty plea.

With both sides recommending the same sentence and with the five years the highest sentence possible, for the four felonies, there was no need to wait, and they were able to do the sentencing that afternoon. Glenn, who did not want to attend, did submit a letter, which the judge read into the record, expressing how violated she felt by what Walter had done to her. Expressing his condemnation, Judge Greenberg, nevertheless, sentenced Walter to what had been agreed. With the sentencing complete, Walter was taken back to the jail to start his sentence, and Sydney headed back toward the office.

———

With Walter's case completed ahead of schedule, Sydney had some time on his hands and coaxed me away from my desk with an invitation to eat lunch down by the river. It's always worthwhile to engage in a conversation with Sydney. I thought I'd ask him the question my father-in-law keeps asking me.

"Congratulations on getting that deal, but don't you ever worry justice isn't being served by what we do? You and I can never fully appreciate the physical aspect of forced and unwanted sex on a woman, but from what you were telling me, your client's crime is going to have a profound and enduring effect on the victim for the rest of her life. You didn't get that plea offer because of any positives on the defense side, but because the victim didn't want to be put through the trauma of being examined and cross-examined about such an intimate thing at a public trial. Is there any way you can say your client got what he deserved?"

"Steve, after years in this business, I think it is foolish to think anyone could ever figure out what the 'right sentence' would be. There is nothing that could be done to Walter that would take Glenn back to her life before the incident happened. The punishment must be defined in terms of time in prison and putting the crime on one side of the scale is not going to magically bring us the amount of time Walter should have served on the other side of the scale.

"Here in Washington State, we long ago gave up the idea that a judge on one end, and a parole board on the other, could evaluate the weight of the defendant's crime and mitigating factors, and decide how long the prison sentence should be. In the 1980s, a Sentencing Guidelines Commission set out to rank felony crimes and assign sentence ranges according to that rank and the defendant's prior felony convictions. If Walter had been convicted of a second-degree rape at that time, his sentence range would only have been 21 to 27 months. Even if the crime had been first-degree rape, where a weapon was used or Glenn was seriously injured, in those days the sentence range would have been 51 to 68 months, just about what Walter is serving for his third-degree rape. However, in 1990, under the effects of early waves of the national "Lock-Them-Up Movement," the legislature decided to increase some of the sentence ranges. If Walter's crime had been committed in the early 90s, his sentence range for second-degree rape would have been that 51 to 68 months. But the legislature was not done. In 1997, with the 'Movement's' biggest waves crashing on Washington's shores, the sentence ranges were upped again, just for sex offenses, so it would now be that 78 to 102 months Walter had originally been facing. Some people might be satisfied the legislature was just correcting and then re-correcting an error.

But for me, once there has been that much politics inserted into deciding what sentence ranges should be, it's definitely not where I need to go to see if Walter got the justice he deserved.

"Looking at a prison sentence as just a number of months is also a distortion, unless one keeps in mind what that means —separation from family, friends and society; and monotonous day after monotonous day after monotonous day as life ticks away. And Walter is going to face more than just that time in prison. He will have to register as a sex offender, his employment possibilities will be tremendously limited, and he will walk out of prison with an incredible debt which will likely follow him his whole life. Accepting that plea offer was Walter's best option, and it accomplished what was best for Glenn and the prosecutor. Accomplishing anything better, a more perfect justice, was never a possibility."

CHAPTER SEVEN
Joe Sellers

Cast of Characters:

Joe Sellers: Defendant

Tony Hawkins: Defense Investigator

Janet Coleman: Prosecutor

Deanna Lacey: Paulson's Date at the Bar

Linda Jenson: Seller's Witness

Laura Berg: Sellers' Lawyer

Judge Dean Jordan: Trial Judge

Bruce Paulson: Crime Victim

Lynn Rice: State's Witness

Steve Cole: Narrator

As if I didn't have enough things on my plate, Laura Berg had come to me asking for help with one of her cases. She had a client that was demanding a new lawyer. While I had had a couple of prior experiences with this situation, Laura had not.

The story of Laura's move into public defense is unique. She was first employed at HCPD as a legal assistant. She was my legal assistant when I was first hired and her knowledge of how to work-the-system kept me out of trouble several times. When she first arrived, she was just completing her bachelor's degree in philosophy and was hoping to go on to graduate school, but over time, her experiences with us led her to decide to become a public defender attorney instead. To achieve that, instead of going to law school, she entered the Washington State's Law Clerk Program, where she was tutored by Jill, our office director. By the time she had completed the program, passed the bar exam, and been sworn in as a lawyer, she was way ahead of the rest of us when we first arrived with nothing but our book learning. One experience she hadn't had was a client who was demanding a new lawyer.

Laura and I walked over to the courthouse and got the jail guards to pull her client out of the collection of inmates waiting for court and place him in a private room. When we entered the room, Laura introduced me to her client, Joe Sellers. I recognized him; that was the guy Laura had tried without success to get released from jail on a lower bail that day I handled the video calendar. The reputation each of us has with our clients frequently depends on how successful we are at things like bail hearings, and despite his extensive criminal record and long history of skipping court, Joe had decided that because Laura had not gotten him released, she was no good.

I observed as Laura asked Joe why he wanted a different lawyer.

"You're not helping me, and my trial is coming up soon."

"Joe," responded Laura. "We are just about prepared for your trial. Our investigator has interviewed all the prosecutor's witnesses, and she is looking for the woman you said you were with when the assault occurred. And I have all the legal issues briefed."

"Well, I don't trust you and I still want another lawyer."

At that point, I interjected.

"Mr. Sellers, it's going to be up to the judge to decide if you get a different lawyer."

"That's not right, they're telling me in the jail that it's my constitutional right to have a lawyer of my choice."

It turns out that is only true for a defendant who can pay for the lawyer they choose. For our public defender clients, they are stuck with the lawyer they draw unless a judge gives them a different one, and that whole process becomes overly complicated. Except in a rare circumstance where an unrepairable mistake is made, the public defender remains as an effective representative for the client, but at the same time the public defender can't defend to the court their ongoing capability to continue representing the client against the claims to the contrary made by the client.

"Joe," Laura said, "we are about to go in front of the judge. If you want a different lawyer, you're going to have to give the judge a reason. I don't know any reason why I can't effectively represent you, so you are going to be the one doing the talking. I can tell you though, I won't say anything to contradict what you say."

Seller's case was soon called, and the jail guards led the three of us into the courtroom where Judge Dean Jordan was presiding. Laura and Joe walked to their place in front of the judge alongside of Janet Coleman, the prosecutor in the case. I moved to the first row of the public seating to watch.

"Ms. Berg, what brings you before the court?"

"Your Honor, my client wishes to ask the court for a new lawyer, and he will be speaking for himself."

"Mr. Sellers," said the judge. "What do you want to tell me?"

"Ms. Berg is not a good lawyer."

"Mr. Sellers, Ms. Berg has appeared in front of me many times and she always did a good job."

"Well, she hasn't done anything good for me. She couldn't get my bail lowered, and they haven't found my witness."

"Mr. Sellers, with your criminal history and your record of failing to appear in court, there is no lawyer that would be able to convince a judge to release you.

"Ms. Berg, what about the witness?"

"We have an investigator looking, Your Honor."

The truth was, we had found the first woman whom Joe claimed would give him an alibi, only to learn he was not with her at that time. Joe gave Laura another name, and that was the one the investigator had not yet been able to find.

"Mr. Sellers," said the judge. "You can't ask for any more than that."

"Well, I just won't work with her."

If a lawyer/client relationship becomes so bad it threatens a fair trial, then a new lawyer has to be appointed, but Joe hadn't demonstrated that, and a judge is not going to allow a defendant to simply refuse to work with one lawyer after another until they get the lawyer they want without giving legally sufficient reasons.

"Mr. Seller," said the judge. "I am not giving you another lawyer. Ms. Berg will effectively represent you."

"But I refuse to work with her. I'll just represent myself."

Whoa. Finding himself boxed in by Judge Jordan's ruling, Joe struck back with the only weapon left to him. He didn't have the right to choose his lawyer, but he did have the right to represent himself.

"Sir, if you are serious about that, you and I are going to need to have a conversation."

Reading from a script, Judge Jordan told Joe, among other things, he was going to be required to follow the rules of evidence and the rules of court procedure. Although he hadn't taken the course on evidence we lawyers got in law school, Joe agreed he could follow the rules, and Judge Jordan allowed him to represent himself. More for the benefit of the court than for Joe's benefit, the judge did appoint Laura to be standby counsel.

As we walked back to the office, Laura had lots of questions. I had been standby counsel in one case and, although, while that trial proceeded, I was never sure I was doing the right thing, I offered Laura some answers.

"Laura, you are basically there to take over the defense if Sellers requests, or if the judge decides he is being too disruptive. You need to be at the trial but say and do nothing unless asked by your client or the judge. And yes, he remains your client, so the rule of confidentiality remains in effect. You should probably go see him a couple of times before trial. And... who is your investigator?"

"Tony."

"Be sure to have him continue looking for that woman Sellers wants to find."

We got back to the office and Laura packed up all the police reports, Tony Hawkins' investigation reports, and all the legal work she had done and sent it over to Joe in the jail. I didn't hear much about the case until two weeks later when the trial had been completed. Laura had quite a story to tell.

—

Joe had been charged with second-degree assault. The allegation was that he had been in a bar by himself, pretty intoxicated. He had leaned over and said something suggestive to a woman named Deanna Lacey, who was sitting at the next table with her date, Bruce Paulson. When Paulson told him in a flurry of expletives to leave them alone, Joe stood up and smashed Paulson in the face with a beer bottle, breaking Paulson's cheekbone. He immediately left the bar and was seen driving off in a gray, older model car. One of the bar patrons who saw the car drive off thought it had a Washington State plate with the letters AFY. However, they had not been able to get any of the numbers.

Nobody at the bar knew the guy who had committed the assault, and the bar had been pretty dark. However, with the help of a couple of the other patrons, Lacey had come up with a general description of the assailant. The police had reviewed the department of licensing records and found three older model gray vehicles with Washington licenses beginning in AFY. The only one in Hudson County belonged to Joe Sellers, who happened to have a criminal record, which included an assault.

When contacted, Joe had denied being the one who committed

the assault. Intelligently, he refused to say anything further until he could talk with an attorney. The police put together a montage of booking photos of six men, including Joe and five others that looked generally like him. They showed the montage individually to Paulson and Lacey. Paulson had failed to identify any of the six pictures. Lacey did pick out Joe's photo and said it looked a lot like the guy, but she couldn't be one hundred percent certain. The bartender couldn't make an identification but was pretty sure the guy wasn't a regular customer. Lynn Rice, who had been alone in a booth near the door, was able to pick out Joe and was "almost positive" he was the guy running out of the tavern.

Laura had really been looking forward to trying this case. Even with just the prosecutor's witnesses, the case had "reasonable doubt" written all over it. With Joe's decision to represent himself, Laura got relegated to the public seating to watch in total frustration what occurred.

The case ended back in Judge Jordan's court for trial. Laura was there waiting when the jail guards brought Joe into the courtroom. He was carrying the defense materials she had sent to him, still bound in their original wrapping, suggesting they hadn't been the subject of much study. HCPD had provided him with some appropriate clothes for trial, and Laura had gone to the jail twice to answer any questions, but Joe had refused to meet with her. As they waited for Coleman to arrive, Laura went up to Joe one more time.

"Joe, do you have any questions for me? It's going to be your case to present, but I am here to answer any questions."

Still filled with anger that had only built up during the last two weeks, Joe responded: "No, leave me alone."

"Can I, at least, tell you what is going to happen here?"

"No."

Having tried her best, Laura retreated to the public seating and sat in silence as Coleman entered and arranged her trial materials on the table before her. It wasn't long before Judge Jordan came in and the case got underway.

"Ms. Coleman," said the judge. "Do you have anything to be considered before we bring in the jury?"

"Yes, Your Honor, Mr. Sellers hasn't provided us with a witness list."

"Mr. Sellers, the prosecutor has the right to know if you have any witnesses other than yourself."

"I don't know yet."

"Well, you are going to have to have a really good reason for not providing that person's name at this time if you decide later you want to call someone. Do you have anything you want the court to decide before we bring in the jury?"

On the advice of somebody in the jail, Joe had decided to ask the judge to prevent the prosecutor from offering evidence of his prior convictions.

"Well, Ms. Coleman, what about criminal history evidence."

"Your Honor, we believe Mr. Sellers' 2016 assault conviction is admissible as modus operandi. It was another fight in a tavern."

Hearing that said, Laura sat up straight with alarm. She had seen this issue out there when she was preparing to be the lawyer and the draft of her brief on this issue was sitting on the table in front of Sellers. Unable to contain herself, she stood.

"Your Honor..."

"Ms. Berg, stop. You are not the lawyer here. Ms. Colman, I am going to be conservative here and not allow this evidence. Fights in bars are all too common. The fact Mr. Sellers was involved in one two years ago does not establish a special pattern to his conduct. It doesn't make it any more likely that of all the people who fight in bars, Mr. Sellers is the person involved in this fight."

Thinking she couldn't have said it better herself, Laura sat down to watch at her ease the proceedings as they continued.

With the preliminaries resolved, the jury pool was brought

in and questioned by the judge, Coleman, and Joe. Laura thought Joe asked some good questions, most particularly whether the jurors thought he was more likely to be guilty because he was representing himself. One of the jurors even thought it might be more likely he was not guilty because he was not hiding behind a lawyer. Coleman exercised a challenge against that juror and another who had served as a bartender in the past. Joe let the jury stand and the trial was underway.

Coleman gave a smooth opening statement in which she acknowledged her witnesses weren't 100 percent sure the picture they'd selected from the montage was the person who had struck the victim, but with all the things corroborating that identification, the jury would be convinced Joseph Sellers was the one who assaulted Bruce Paulson. Joe was short and to the point: "I didn't do this."

Bruce Paulson was Coleman's first witness. He hadn't noticed the person sitting at the table next to his until that person leaned over and made a sexually charged remark to his date of the night, Deanna Lacey. He admitted he had sworn at the guy telling him to leave them alone but had never gotten out of his seat when he was smashed along the side of his face with a beer bottle, at which time he collapsed to the floor. Lacey had knelt beside him and held his hand and shoulder while the bartender brought an ice pack to put on his wound. He had been taken to the hospital where it was determined he had suffered a broken left cheek and, because it distorted his eye socket, he had experienced double vision for a while. The happy news out of this incident was that although this had been his first date with Ms. Lacey, in succeeding weeks, they had developed a relationship and were going to get married. He acknowledged he hadn't been able to identify Joe's photograph from the montage, but on looking across the courtroom, he testified that Mr. Sellers looked a lot like the picture he had in his mind of the guy who'd hit him.

It became time for Joe to cross examine Paulson and, as she sat and watched, Laura went over the questions she would have asked if she'd been the lawyer: the low lights in the bar; the fact that he was facing away from the assailant's table and had only partially turned his head to curse at guy; that he didn't actually see the person when he was being struck; and that he went right to the floor and never saw the assailant after that. However, Joe didn't address any of those factors. He only questioned Paulson on the fact that his wounds had healed, and he was back to being able to do what he wanted.

Deanna Lacey was the next witness. She testified that from her seat at the table, she was not looking at the assailant, but when she heard him start to speak, she turned her head to the left—past Paulson and looked directly into the face of the assailant. She had turned away but did look back when the guy stood up with the beer bottle and struck Paulson. In talking about the montage, Lacey testified that Joe's picture looked most like her memory of the assailant but, as she had said in her written witness statement, she couldn't be 100 percent sure that picture was of the assailant. In looking at the defendant in person in the courtroom, she was a little more convinced that Joe was the one who had assaulted Paulson.

Laura had a similar set of questions in mind for Lacey. The fact she was more certain when seeing Sellers in person had to be understood in the context of his being the only suspect in the courtroom with every finger pointing at him. Joe did get her to repeat she was still not 100 percent sure.

Lynn Rice, who had been seated next to the door, testified she heard a commotion and saw a person run past her out the door. When the bartender had yelled to "see where that guy goes", she had gone to door and seen the guy get into an older model gray car and drive away. She could see the car had what looked like a Washington State license plate starting with the letters AFY, but she did not see what the following numbers were. When asked about her identification of the photograph in the montage, she repeated what she'd said in her witness statement, that she was almost positive he was the person she had seen that night. Unlike Paulson and Lacey, she was not more convinced of her identification by seeing Joe in person. Joe had no questions.

The rest of the testimony offered by Coleman was not controversial. One of the police officers responding to the 911 call testified about what he'd observed on arrival. Paulson's doctor testified about Paulson's broken cheekbone. And a representative from the Department of Licensing testified that a gray 2003 Toyota Corolla with a license number AYF 8254 was registered to Joseph Sellers. With all her evidence in, Colman rested and because it was near the end of the day, Judge Jordan adjourned the trial until the next morning.

The judge and his court staff, and Coleman and Joe sat in silence as the jurors collected their gear from the jury room and left. When the door closed behind the last of them, Judge Jordan addressed Joe.

"Mr. Sellers, your case starts first thing tomorrow. Do you have any witnesses to call besides yourself?"

"I don't know yet."

"Sir," the judge responded somberly, "if you were a lawyer and showed up with a new witness tomorrow, I'd be finding you in contempt of court and imposing a big fine. But, because you don't have a lawyer's experience with court proceedings, I'm going to wait until tomorrow and see what happens. If you do identify a witness, I want that person here first thing."

With that, the judge and his staff went back into chambers; Colman packed up and left the courtroom, and the jail guards came to take Joe away. Laura offered to visit Joe to plan his defense, but he waved her off.

—

Given the quantity of her participation during the first day of trial, Laura decided to bring her laptop and try to get some work done on a brief due by week's end. As she walked into the courtroom, she passed a young woman who asked her if this was where the Sellers case was happening, and Laura confirmed it was. The first day of trial hadn't been attended by anyone who wasn't directly involved in it. At first, Laura thought this must be a student assigned to come watch some court proceedings, but the woman knew the name of the case, so she inquired.

"I am supposed to be a witness."

Laura was surprised but not being on the frontline in this case she decided to let it go until the real players appeared.

Coleman soon arrived and came over to talk to Laura.

"No, Janet. I've been carefully schooled that as standby counsel I can't say or listen to anything about the case without Mr. Sellers being present." With an increased sense of anticipation, Laura returned to her place in the public seating to wait for the rest of the players.

When Joe was brought in, Coleman walked over to talk to him, but Laura intervened, suggesting whatever she meant to say should probably be done in front of the judge and on the record. The expectation of something big made waiting for the judge seem longer than it was, but Judge Jordan did finally appear.

"Your Honor," Coleman began. "We are moving to reopen our case. We obtained evidence last night that Mr. Sellers phoned someone named Linda Jensen and promised her his brother Jim Sellers would pay $5,000 if she'd testify that she and the defendant had been on a date the night of this assault. As with all calls from jail directed to someone other than an attorney, this call was recorded and we're prepared to call an official from the jail to authenticate it as having been one of these recorded calls and had been made with Mr. Seller's pin number, from his unit in the jail. The recorded conversation made references to an ongoing trial in front of you, Your Honor, and the date of assault on Mr. Paulson is the date the caller referenced. I have reason to believe the woman sitting here is Ms. Jensen."

On hearing that, one of the jail guards moved over near to the woman to discourage her from leaving.

"Miss," the judge spoke in her direction, "you need to stay here, but I am telling you not to say anything until you have an opportunity to speak to a lawyer." With that, the judge's law clerk walked to the next courtroom where there were active proceedings and persuaded one of the waiting lawyers to come talk to the woman. When the lawyer arrived, he and the woman went out into the hall, and, in short order, the lawyer came back into the courtroom, announcing that the woman wasn't going to participate in the proceedings.

Anticipating there might be some things to discuss before the trial restarted, Judge Jordan had set the return time for the jury at 10 o'clock. However, at that point, some jurors had begun to appear, and the law clerk was dispatched to collect the jury in a courtroom down the hall. Joe's frustration and anger increased minute by minute as the morning's events proceeded, but he'd remained silently sitting in his chair until it had been announced that the woman had left.

"Your Honor, this isn't fair--"

"Mr. Sellers," interrupted the judge. "You need to stop talking. Anything you say or do at this point can be used against you in this trial.

"Please take Mr. Sellers and Ms. Berg to some place where they can talk in private.

"We are in recess."

When Laura entered the room where they had taken Joe, she anticipated she would again be told not to get involved. Instead,

Joe looked over at her in obvious frustration.

"Ms. Berg, what can I do? That was my friend Linda; she was coming to testify that we were together on the night of the assault."

"Joe, with the evidence that the prosecutor has, the jury would never believe her, and she'd be committing several crimes if she did testify. Leaving was the right move for her."

"What about the money Jim paid her?"

"Joe don't drag me any deeper into this mess. That is between the three of you and has nothing to do with your trial. You are still in control of this case, and you need to decide where to go from here."

"I don't know what to do; I want you to represent me now."

Laura didn't have any idea what to do either, but she knew if Joe asked, the judge would put her back in charge of the defense case.

"Joe, just tell the judge that's what you want."

Back in the courtroom, Judge Jordan granted Joe's request to have Laura take over the defense, and her first move was to ask for a mistrial. There were countless questions she'd have wanted to ask the prosecutor's witnesses on cross-examination, and there was this new debacle for which a strategy needed to be developed. That motion was denied. Laura well knew a person who represents themself can't claim ineffective assistance of counsel for what they did or didn't do at trial, even if they were representing themselves for only a part of the trial. As a result, there was no basis for a mistrial. Failing that, Laura asked for a recess until the next day. Judge Jordan denied that but did agree to recess the case for the rest of the morning.

Together in private, Laura and Joe tried to figure out what to do. As things stood, there was no favorable evidence for the defense. The biggest question was whether Joe could possibly testify. If he did, Laura explained, he'd be asked if he'd made that call to Jensen. If he chose to deny it, he could be prosecuted for perjury.

On top of that, he could only offer that answer in a response to a question from the prosecutor, because as his attorney she was not allowed to facilitate a client's lie to the court. If he did testify, it would be better to admit he'd make the call, but that would only be more evidence he was guilty of witness tampering.

After the lunch break, Colman was allowed to reopen her case and, after satisfying the requirements for its admissibility, played for the jury the recording of Joe's phone call to Jensen.

Joe had decided he would testify and after Coleman rested her case again, he took the witness stand. His story was he had never been in that bar and did not assault Mr. Paulson. When told by the police at the time of his arrest a month after the incident what the date was, he was not able to figure out where he was at that time. On cross-examination, he admitted asking his friend Linda Jensen to come testify he was with her that night but, nevertheless, reaffirmed that those witnesses from the bar had made a mistake Under questioning from Laura, he told the jury he'd asked Jensen to lie for him because he was afraid of going to prison but he really didn't assault Mr. Paulson.

Closing arguments followed. Coleman told the jury that although no one witness was absolutely certain Sellers was the assailant, the combination of the identifications made by the three witnesses together with the link to Sellers' car gave the jury a firm basis to conclude it was he who committed this assault. If that testimony left the jury with any doubts, the defendant's call to his friend trying to get her to give him an alibi was, in essence, his admission of guilt.

Laura stood to respond, but all the questions Joe had failed to ask the witnesses showing the limited time and opportunity they'd had to observe the assailant left her with little to say. Her major talking point was that the month between the incident and his arrest had left Mr. Sellers no way to figure out where he had actually been that night. Trying to get his friend to say they were together was wrong, but he had done that because of his fear of being wrongfully convicted and going to prison and not out of a consciousness of guilt.

Coleman was not long with her rebuttal argument. The jury went into the jury room to deliberate but returned in a matter of minutes with a guilty verdict. Joe's frustration and anger resurfaced, and he again fired Laura. She was nevertheless in court two days later to witness Judge Jordan sentence Sellers to 17 months in prison, the high end of the standard range. Coleman indicated her office had decided not to pursue the witness tampering charge against Joe or any kind of attempted perjury against Ms. Jensen.

No effort was made to find out what happened to the $5,000.

CHAPTER EIGHT

The Pretrial Battles

Jeff had talked to the police about the incident on two occasions, and what he said could be used against him in his trial unless the police were acting illegally in obtaining those statements. The things he admitted to in those statements weren't too harmful to our case, but the words he used in explaining his hands around Darlene's neck had me a little worried.

Litigating issues like this is almost always done before the trial starts. Decisions on questions of this sort are made by the judge and resolving them in advance avoids interruptions during the presentation to the jury. At Jeff's omnibus hearing, we scheduled a hearing to contest the admissibility of these statements.

Ours was not the only case scheduled for a pretrial hearing on this date. There were 20 other cases scheduled. Most of them were stricken because the prosecutor and defense attorney had reached an agreement on a plea bargain or, if the case was still headed for trial, an agreement about the admissibility of the evidence. There were, however, several cases, including ours, that had to be decided and we were going to have to wait our turn. I arrived a few minutes ahead of the start of court and spoke briefly to Jeff, who was there in handcuffs attached to a chain around his waist and sitting in the jury box alongside several other defendants similarly bound. I then went over to sit in the public seating with Joyce Benson and George Sanders, who were also scheduled for hearings. Howard Graham had a case scheduled too, the first one on the list, but, as usual, he had not yet arrived.

At the stroke of the hour Judge Greenberg entered the courtroom and called the first case. "State v. Kevin O'Reilly."

I remembered that case. That was the defendant at the Omnibus Hearing when Howard had missed court. Knowing Howard, I was guessing he'd made up to O'Reilly with a lot of big promises and today was going to be the day he was supposed to produce on those.

"Where is Mr. Graham," asked the judge. Just at that moment, the courtroom door swung open loudly and Howard walked in.

"I'm here, Your Honor, we'll be ready to go in just a minute." Howard went to the counsel table and began to assemble his paperwork. The jail guards brought O'Reilly over to sit beside him and it appeared to us in the audience that he and Howard had developed a reasonably workable relationship. Keith White, the prosecutor handling the case, had long been in place at his table with the two officers who had arrested O'Reilly.

O'Reilly had been charged with possession of a stolen firearm and, being forbidden to possess firearms because of a prior felony conviction, he was also being charged with unlawful possession of a firearm. Howard had talked about this case at one of our felony meetings. He was going to argue O'Reilly's arrest, when the stolen gun was found under his seat in the car, was illegal and, therefore, the testimony of the arresting officer must be suppressed. If that argument succeeded, the prosecutor's whole case would collapse and O'Reilly would walk free.

Once Howard was settled, White stood and called Officer Foster to the stand. Howard asked the judge to order that while one officer was testifying, the other should leave the courtroom and that the two should not discuss their testimony with one another until the court had made its ruling. The judge agreed and Officer Hatch left the courtroom as Foster took the stand.

Officer Foster testified he and Officer Hatch had been parked near an intersection at about 2 a.m. and had observed a car make a right turn without signaling. They decided to stop the car. After the car pulled over, he approached the driver's window and observed the driver Kevin O'Reilly fumbling for something in the glove compartment. Concerned for his safety, he asked O'Reilly to get out of the car and while he was examining O'Reilly's driver's license, Officer Hatch took a flashlight, looked inside the vehicle, and observed the handle of a pistol sticking out from underneath the driver's seat. When the computer showed O'Reilly had a prior felony conviction, he was arrested.

When White finished his examination, Howard began his cross. Joyce, George, and I had been looking forward to this. Howard fumbles a lot of balls in the course of his work, but at cross-examination, he is a star.

"Officer Foster, how many cars did you see go through this intersection while you were stationed there?"

"I can't tell you the number."

"Was it a lot, just a few, or something in between?"

"There weren't many cars that time of night."

"Were there any vehicles following Mr. O'Reilly's as he made that right turn or any in the lane into which he turned?"

"No."

"Were you assigned to do traffic control at that intersection at 2 a.m.?

"No, we were looking for illegal drug activity. We've had a lot of complaints about that in this neighborhood."

"You testified that Mr. O'Reilly failed to signal for a right turn. Was he speeding?"

"No."

"Was he weaving across lanes?"

"No."

"Did he have a headlight or a taillight out?"

"No."

"Just failing to signal?"

"Yes."

"Did Mr. O'Reilly show any hostility towards you when you approached his car."

"No, but I was concerned when I saw him reaching into his glove compartment."

"Is that why you asked him to step out of the car?"

"Yes."

"You had asked him for his license and proof of insurance?"

"Yes."

"And in your time as a police officer you have known drivers to keep that information in their glove compartment."

"Yes, but it was late at night, and this was a high crime area."

"Did you ever check the glove compartment?"

"No, that wasn't necessary because we had the man in custody."

"Thank you, Officer Foster."

White had no questions on re-direct. Officer Foster left the witness stand, and, as Officer Hatch entered the courtroom and took his place on the witness stand, Foster left the room in compliance with the court's requirement.

Officer Hatch told pretty much the same story. She had remained in the police car while Officer Foster contacted O'Reilly. But it was she who took the flashlight and looked into the car. She testified she had not entered the vehicle, but the driver's door had been left open, and she could see the handle of a gun sticking out from underneath the driver's seat.

Crime training 101: if an officer asks you to get out of your car, shut the door behind you. White's examination of this officer didn't take long. As Howard stood and approached the witness, his obvious enthusiasm caught the attention of all of us in the public seating.

"Officer Hatch, you had contact with Mr. O'Reilly prior to the time of this arrest?"

"Yes."

Wow, that was going to be an important piece of the story.

"You had been involved in an arrest of Mr. O'Reilly in this same vehicle two months earlier. It was you who signed him to the Hudson County Jail, and you were involved in the further investigation of that case."

"Yes, that is true."

"When did you tell Officer Foster you knew whom you had stopped?"

"When the car had stopped, I recognized it from our earlier arrest and told Officer Foster."

"And Officer Foster knew whom he was dealing with when he made his first contact with Mr. O'Reilly."

"Yes."

"Thank, you Officer Hatch."

White had no other witnesses and rested. Howard offered no testimony and told the judge he was prepared to make his argument.

"Your Honor, the evidence obtained by Officers Foster and Hatch must be suppressed because it was taken in violation of the defendant's constitutional rights. The officers were using Mr. O'Reilly's failure to signal as a pretext for stopping him. The only thing he did wrong was failing to signal; he wasn't speeding; he wasn't weaving, suggesting a possible DUI; and there was nothing wrong with his vehicle. His failing to signal had no negative consequences because there was no one on the road to receive the signal. Officers Foster and Hatch were not on patrol to monitor the traffic; they were on the watch for criminal activity. They stopped Mr. O'Reilly because he was the only one on the road at 2 a.m. and they wanted to see if he was involved in something criminal.

"What makes the illegality of this arrest more obvious is that before officer Foster got out of his car to approach O'Reilly's car, he had learned whom he was dealing with. So instead of saying, 'Hey buddy, you failed to signal. Be more careful next time' and then letting him go, which I suggest would be the most reasonable response in this situation, Officer Hatch continued to detain Mr. Reilly.

"Then, instead of receiving Mr. O'Reilly's license and proof of insurance and issuing him a ticket through the driver side window as state law requires, he makes an additional intrusion into Mr. O'Reilly's constitutional rights by ordering him out of the car, the direct consequence of which was that Officer Hatch's flashlight search discovered the pistol that has become the basis for the charges here. The testimony of these two officers should be suppressed and the pistol not admitted into evidence."

White responded. "Your Honor, the law that requires a person to signal when making a right turn does not offer any exceptions. The defendant failed to signal and was subject to being stopped because of it. Officer Foster was justified in ordering Mr. O'Reilly out of the car and Officer Hatch was justified in her flashlight search because it was 2 a.m. in a high crime area and the officers knew they were dealing with a law breaker who had been seen fumbling in his glove compartment."

"Anything further Mr. Graham?"

"Your Honor, Mr. O'Reilly didn't lose his constitutional rights because he was driving at 2 a.m. through a high crime neighborhood, even if he had a criminal history. We can never get into the brain of the officer to know for sure what they are thinking, but the law regarding pretext stops doesn't require that. All the facts in this case lead to the inescapable conclusion this was a pretext stop.

Judge Greenberg spent a few moments reading through his

notes and appeared to jot down a few words. He then lifted his head and made his ruling:

"The officers were exercising their lawful authority when they stopped Mr. O'Reilly after he failed to signal. Mr. White is right, there are no exceptions, it is a violation of the law to fail to signal even if there is no other vehicle that needs to see it."

"Oh shit," I thought. *The judge isn't going to see what was so obvious to us, that the police used that failure to signal as a pretext to stop someone they wanted to investigate for more serious criminal activity.* But then Judge Greenberg continued.

"Stopping Mr. O'Reilly was within the law and Officer Foster's approach to the driver's window was within the law, but ordering him to get out of the car, which then facilitated Officer Hatch's search, was a violation of Mr. O'Reilly's rights. Officer Hatch had the authority to obtain Mr. O'Reilly's driver's license and proof of insurance and to write him a ticket, all of which could be done through the driver's side window. Mr. Graham was right. Mr. O'Reilly's rights were not reduced because he was driving in a high crime neighborhood at 2 a.m. The gun and all testimony about its discovery are inadmissible.

We continued to sit silently, but Joyce punched me in the shoulder signaling her pleasure, which George and I shared, about Howard's victory. It occurred to me as I thought about it, Judge Greenberg's ruling gave Howard his win without having to accuse the officers of fabricating a basis for the stop.

—

George's case was called next, and Joyce's followed, but the facts and law were clearly on the side of the prosecutors and they both went down to defeat. They could have saved time by simply agreeing with the prosecutor to a decision that looked inevitable. However, a defendant has the right to have everything contested and bringing a client to a pre-trial hearing gives the client a bit of a preview of what the full trial would be like, which can help a client make better decisions about their case.

Jeff's case was next. I moved over to counsel table and Jeff was brought to join me. Officers Fleming and Brown, who had made the original arrest, and Detective Gray, who had interrogated Jeff later in the jail, had been waiting all morning. They joined Winston at the prosecutor's table. Winston was seeking to offer as evidence at trial both what Jeff had said to Fleming and Brown and his more detailed statement to Gray. Although arguments about the two statements would be different, Judge Greenberg asked us to present all the testimony before any arguments were presented.

Officer Fleming took the stand and, as was done in the O'Reilly case, Brown and Gray headed for the hall. Officer Fleming testified he and Officer Brown had been dispatched to respond to a call about an assault. They went to the home of a Mary Jordan where Ms. Jordan told them she had heard her neighbor Darlene Harris screaming. She had escorted Ms. Harris into her apartment, where she heard Ms. Harris say her husband had choked her. The Officers then talked to Darlene Harris who was extremely upset and crying but had managed to tell them her husband had come home angry and had held her around the neck until she broke free, and at some point, when her husband's hands were around her neck, she couldn't catch a breath. Fleming testified he and Brown then went next door and had Mr. Harris step outside where he was detained.

Winston then asked, "What was Mr. Harris' emotional state?"

"He was very upset."

"Did he say anything?"

"When we asked him what happened, he said he had strangled his wife."

Wait a minute! This was the first time Officer Fleming had

ever indicated Jeff had said he "strangled" his wife. It wasn't in his report where Fleming had written that Jeff had only admitted to putting his hands around her neck, and it hadn't been said to our investigator during their interview. Fleming was trying to make the prosecutor's case stronger than it was. It also wasn't in Officer Brown's written report or in his interview with our investigator.

Winston completed his direct examination and, anxious to get moving, I started my cross.

"You wrote a report shortly after arresting Mr. Harris, right?"

"Yes."

"And in that report, you describe what Mr. Harris said to you?"

"Yes."

"And nowhere in that description did you use the word 'strangulation?'"

Officer Fleming spent half a minute looking through his report, then admitted he hadn't.

"As a result of your interviews with Ms. Harris and Ms. Jordan," I continued, "didn't you come to believe you had developed probable cause to conclude that Mr. Harris had assaulted his wife."

"Yes."

"Did you think the assault was a felony?"

"Well yes, it was a case of strangulation."

"You knew this was a case of alleged domestic violence?"

"Yes."

"And you knew that, because this was domestic violence, the law was requiring you to take Mr. Harris into custody?"

"Yes."

"But you didn't advise Mr. Harris of his Miranda Rights?

"No, but we hadn't taken him into custody when we asked him to tell us what happened."

"But when you walked away from Ms. Jordan's house you and Officer Brown had decided you were going to arrest Mr. Harris?"

"Yes."

"Your Honor, I have no further questions at this point."

On re-direct, Winston asked, "Was Mr. Harris in handcuffs when he was asked what happened?"

"No."

"And he was on his own front porch when he made that admission?"

"Yes."

It was time for Officer Brown to testify. His story was about the same as Fleming's. On cross-examination, I did get him to say when Jeff came out onto the porch, he had slipped between Jeff and the door while Officer Fleming stood at the head of the stairs leading to the street blocking him from retreating into his house or running away.

Winston next called Detective Gray. There wasn't much wrong with most of what Jeff had said to her, but he did say to her that Darlene's spending the money for Christi's shoes and coat was going to mean he would be going to jail. We were trying to stay away from any connection between Jeff and jail that might lead a jury to do more speculating about what kind of life he had lived, a particular problem when his credibility as a witness was going to be so critical to our case.

Detective Gray testified she'd contacted Jeff in the jail the morning after his arrest. She had definitely advised him of the Miranda warning that anything he said to her could be used against him in court and that he had a right to remain silent and to consult with an attorney before and during the making of any statement. She went on to say Jeff agreed to waive his rights and went ahead to make a recorded statement in response to her interrogation. I had no cross-examination and Winston rested his presentation of evidence.

Judge Greenberg addressed Jeff directly, advising him he could testify here and anything he said could not be used against him in trial. We had already decided Jeff would not testify here. We had what we needed for my argument about the statements to Officers Fleming and Brown, and we weren't going to risk having Jeff testify about his statement to Detective Gray. Although what he said at this hearing couldn't be presented as evidence in the prosecutor's case, anything he said could be used as impeachment if it contradicted anything he did say at trial.

I did have one witness to present, Eric Scanlan. He was the public defender assigned to receive random calls from anyone with a criminal law question on the afternoon Jeff had been arrested. Jeff had called and Eric had told him that a public defender was being appointed to represent him and that he should definitely not speak to anyone about his case until the lawyer comes to talk to him. My purpose for calling Eric was to form a basis for a rather way-out argument regarding the admissibility of Jeff's statement to Detective Gray.

Figuring out where I was going, Winston called back Detective Gray and she testified Jeff had never mentioned he had talked to a public defender and had never said he wanted the assistance of a lawyer.

It was now time for argument. Judge Greenberg said he wanted to deal with the statement to Detective Gray first. I argued Jeff had obtained the representation of a lawyer, and hearing from the detective that he had the right to have a lawyer present could have reasonably led him to assume one of the public defenders would have been present when he made his statement.

Winston stood to speak, but Judge Greenberg cut him off.

"I am ready to rule. Mr. Cole, Detective Gray fully advised Mr. Harris of his rights. Mr. Harris could see there was no lawyer present and had been told under such circumstances he had the right to remain silent. Harris' statement to Detective Gray is admissible. Now what about the statement to the two officers. Mr. Cole."

"Your Honor, Officers Fleming and Brown had probable cause to arrest Mr. Harris when they first contacted him. Because they were dealing with an allegation of felony domestic violence, the officers were going to be required to take him into custody. Mr. Harris was not free to go when the officers took positions preventing him from going back into his house or heading down to the street. They nevertheless chose to ask him what happened without ever advising him of his Miranda rights. That makes what Mr. Harris said inadmissible at his trial.

Winston argued this was a "Terry Stop" where the officers didn't have probable cause for the arrest, but only a reasonable suspicion. I responded the officers admitted they had probable cause. Winston started to offer further argument, but Judge Greenberg held up his hand and said he was ready to rule.

"I am going to rule that Mr. Harris' statement to Officers Fleming and Brown is inadmissible. The officers had more than a 'reasonable suspicion.' As they said themselves, they had probable cause to arrest Mr. Harris. They were in fact detaining him from the moment they took positions to prevent him from leaving their company and should have advised him of his Miranda rights before asking him what had happened."

Having obtained half of what we wanted, the only half we had much of a chance with, I told Jeff I would see him soon, and as the jail guards took him away, I packed up and headed back to the office.

CHAPTER NINE

The Trouble with Public Defense

Polly called and asked me to come over to her office. When I arrived, George Sanders was there with her. They had been having an in-depth discussion about public defense and they wanted my opinion. George was talking about his frustration with the work.

"I took this job," he was saying, "because I wanted to take on the evil giants that were holding down justice and make this a better world. But all I have been able to do here is to help my clients one by one get the best result possible within their specific circumstances. Prison sentences are still far too long, and there are nowhere near enough programs available during those sentences or afterward to help people to avoid ending up back there as repeat offenders. Even before they get convicted, people without resources are held in jail until their trial. We don't do near enough with drug court and other therapeutic specialty courts, and entrance into those courts is controlled by the prosecutors with little sensitivity to the needs of those seeking admission. I was actually more content with the criminal justice system before I started working here and came to see how bad things were."

"Couldn't you find Sydney," I asked Polly.

"No, he's gone for the day. George has promised to track him down later, but, Steve, you have been working here a while and I thought you might have an answer.

Polly turned back to George, "I too can feel the injustices we are living under, but I wouldn't think of leaving this place. Every call from a client is an opportunity to help that inspires me to kick a lawyer in the butt to go see them in jail or to renegotiate a plea deal with the prosecutor and I get real satisfaction because I know, whether the client appreciates or not, we did everything we could for them. We are kind of like the Sisters in Mother Teresa's Missionaries of Charity working with the poor in the streets of Calcutta."

"Oh, come on Polly," I said. "There are no saints around here."

"No one knows that better than me, Steve."

A lot of us here have had thoughts like George, including me, and moving on to a job more focused on changing policy than individual representation had proven to be a good path for some.

"George, did you know Marian Austin when she worked here? She left after three years to join a non-profit organization involved in litigation about the conditions of Washington State prison inmates. She likes what she is doing and thinks they had been able to put pressure on the legislature and department of corrections to expand college course offerings."

"I think that might be the right path for me at this point," said George. "It would mean an opportunity to have a real effect on the criminal justice system and fewer trips to the jail. I bet I would be operating under a lot less pressure than I am here."

"Well George, if you do go in that direction, I bet you will arrive in a better position to understand what you should be working for because of your experiences here."

"For sure!"

—

The next day, I was just back from the jail, walking down the hall to my office, when I saw several of our lawyers in Anita Carter's office. As I passed, Laura Berg asked me to join.

"Anita says she's got to quit. She can't afford to stay on the salary she is getting."

Anita had been talking to a lot of us about her struggle. She had finished college with a pretty significant debt and only tripled the total in law school. Her law school had set the payments at what she could afford because she was working in public defense, but she was just barely keeping ahead of the interest. In various degrees this is a problem a lot of our lawyers have.

"Anita, what's going on?" I asked.

"My partner and I have been thinking about what we want to do with our lives together from here. We've been thinking about having a child and buying a house within a reasonable distance of her work and mine. I've looked at the salary scale here and even if I get to the higher levels, we won't be able to accomplish those things, not because we couldn't have a house and kids with the salaries we're getting, but adding my school debt and her school debt makes that impossible.

"I've been talking to the people at 'Hegge and Galloway.' They offered me a nice raise and would set me up to do some business law and wills and estate planning with a partnership down the road which is going to work out financially and give me some time away to spend with a child."

"But you won't be going to court, and you won't have any cops to cross-examine."

"I know, and I am going to miss it, and I am going to miss being here with my fellow warriors."

It occurred to me how lucky I had been to have two parents with professional careers who helped me through college and law school. I had walked out of law school with what I thought was a lot of debt, but not so much that I wasn't able to stay on top of it and go to work where I wanted. I remember back in law school talking to classmates who went into law because they wanted to get into court. Some wanted to be defense attorneys and some prosecutors. As it turned out, so many of them couldn't afford to take those jobs because the salaries didn't let them pay off their student loans. I remember my dad telling me his cost to go to the University of Washington law school was ten percent of what it had cost me to go to the same school twenty years later, after consideration of inflation. Along with failing to care for the medical needs of its people or doing anything to address climate change, America is failing to provide for the education of its youth.

It was closing in on the end of the day. Others had finished working and had come over to join in, soon overflowing Anita's office out into the hall. Eric Scanlan was one of the newly hired lawyers at HCPD. He'd come to us after completing a clerkship at the state Court of Appeals, and we were looking to him, along with his trial work, as a resource for caselaw, opinions from the appellate courts we needed for arguments in our cases we didn't always have time to find for ourselves. Upon hearing about Anita's situation, he joined the conversation.

"I'm worried about that too. I really like what I am doing now. For the first time in my legal career, I get to help real people with real legal problems and have the full responsibility doing it. I figure I can hang on for a couple of years, but unless things change for me too, I will probably have to look for something else as well."

Several other lawyers, while seeming to have their financial situations under control, did express concerns about our public defender salaries and everyone agreed it was a problem. Criminal defense is not a branch of the law where the skills can be fully honed in a couple of years; it's a career mired in more complex issues of constitutional law than other branches of the law and requires highly developed communication skills necessary for daily presentations to judges and juries. There are a few lawyers who go into private practice doing criminal defense and make a good income. However, the Bureau of Justice Statistics has determined that 82 percent of people being charged with crimes are indigent and need to have a public defender lawyer. Justice needs career public defenders.

Everybody wanted to hear what Sydney Johnson had do say. This time he was here when we needed him.

"You know things here used to be a lot worse," he began. "Hudson County used to contract with individual lawyers at a set fee per case and the money was so bad only new lawyers would take the cases and most of the defendants pled guilty because that was the easiest way for the lawyer to get the fee. Now we have a public defender office with full-time lawyers being paid regular salaries assisted by investigators, social workers, and office staff."

"Yeah," Joyce Benson spoke up. "We might have left the dark ages behind, but we still don't have enough lawyers to handle the cases we are taking on and we are not able to get investigators and social workers assigned to our cases because they are drowning in the cases they are already working on."

Joyce was probably the most meticulous lawyer at HCPD. She carried around in her head a quite complete knowledge of all her cases, including all the upcoming court dates for each. The investigators and social workers enjoyed being assigned to one of her cases because she would bring them in early and give them a clear picture of what needed to be done. It was a surprise to us all when she got fined by the court for not being ready for trial when it was scheduled to start. However, it was a surprise to no one, when at a motion for reconsideration, she got the judge to reverse himself by presenting her email chains, showing early requests and late responses for interviews with the police investigators and similar delays by the prosecutor in arranging the interview with the complaining witness.

"I just finished reading *Just Mercy*," she continued, "a book by Bryan Stevenson about guys he saved from the death penalty. They'd been represented by lawyers decades before who just let their innocent clients get convicted and sent off to death row, and I don't want to look back in ten years to find that an innocent person went to prison because I had too many other cases to give them the defense they needed."

"That will always be a concern," Sydney responded, "but those people Stevenson was writing about were African-Americans in cases that went to trial decades ago in the deep south where every dimension of the court system was racist. I'm certainly not defending everything that goes on in Hudson County against claims of racism, but our courts and prosecutors aren't consciously racist, and it is a big part of our job to expose any systemic racism where it creeps in. Joyce, I think when you are talking to your grandchildren about what you did back in the day, you will be proud."

"Sydney," replied Joyce. "You know there is a lot more to our job than winning an acquittal for an innocent client. Every one of our clients deserves our hands-on treatment, and there just aren't enough hours in the day to do all that with the number of cases we are being assigned."

All eyes focused on Sydney for an answer.

"I am not trying to say the limitations we work under are fair. Like the rest of you, I wake up nights worrying about things I didn't have enough time to get done; about the lack of enough investigators and social workers to prepare our cases; and about the fact we have many fewer office staff positions than the prosecutor's office... even though we are the ones dealing with actual clients in the thousands. If you want to march to the courthouse and wave signs demanding all those things we need, I will be with you. But even if you were to get some help with the things you need, it will never be enough. We are better off here in Washington than public defenders in most other states, because our Supreme Court set those caseload standards, so you guys can't do more than 150 felonies in a year. Most states don't' have caseload standards and their public defenders are doing way more than 150 cases."

Joyce wasn't satisfied.

"I can't imagine having to triage a caseload of 250 cases to find the few clients to whom I can bring a little bit of justice, leaving the rest to the mercy of the prosecutor's plea offer. The lawyers doing that have my profound sympathy. The problem here is that a caseload standard of 150 felonies doesn't work either. I am taking on too many overly complicated cases with horrendous consequences for the client to be able to effectively represent the rest of my 150. Those standards created by the court allow all the counties to self-righteously think they're assuring justice so long as we each don't do more than 150 cases a year."

"There are always a couple of things I like to keep in mind," said Sydney. "What we do is fundamentally competitive. We try to beat the prosecutors when we go to trial. Even when a case ends in a guilty plea, we want to do better than the prosecutor's first offer. When a judge denies a motion, we want to make the record strong enough so that the appellate court might reverse the judge's decision. But one part of any competition is a constant thought that there is something more that can be done. So, like a sports team or an army at war, you are never going to think you are fully prepared.

"Having said that, I agree with all of you. With the number of lawyers, investigators, social workers, and office staff we have, we will never be as prepared for our combat as are the Seahawks

113

or the US Army for theirs. And that can affect us in our sense of achievement and our value of ourselves. But your sense of self-value should get fully reinstated when you realize how absolutely critical it is that we are there to do what we do in the criminal justice system in this country. If we all quit because we had too many cases and not enough investigators, social workers, and office staff to do our work to the level we thought was right, then we would be replaced by people who are perfectly satisfied with the job they are doing and would keep the system plugging along. Then, in another three decades, Bryan Stevenson's granddaughter would be here in Washington State freeing innocent people after thirty years of unjust incarceration."

Sydney's comments seemed to quell the level of anxiety, although several in the group did walk away resolved to go see the head of our office to make sure that the county government was fully aware of our level of dissatisfaction. It was the end of the workday and the group broke up, some going home but some back to their offices to finish up a few things.

—

I have long considered myself fully committed to my work as a public defender. Yes, there have been too many cases and not enough help, but that only inspired me to work harder and be more creative. My bigger concerns these days have to do with the other dimensions of my life. I have always enjoyed hiking and camping. Every summer, for as long as I can remember, my parents, my two sisters and I would go on a week-long hiking and camping trip into the mountains, along a river, or beside the ocean. When I got my driver's license and permission to use one of the family cars, I took solo trips for a day, sometimes two, and went hiking along a trail somewhere. That hiking became running, and over the years, I logged thousands of miles among the trees, high into the mountains, and along the crashing waves of an ocean beach. In college, I joined a hiking club and went with the group on weekend excursions. I met my wife Stephanie on an outing with that group and it wasn't long before she and I would go out on our own. Our love of the outdoors was a big part of why we were drawn together.

Stephanie and I got married right after I graduated from college with a major in sociology. She had two more years to go, and I went on to law school. When Stephanie graduated with an education degree, she got a job as a 4th grade public school teacher. A year later, I graduated from law school, took the Washington State Bar Exam, and became a lawyer. During these years, one of the things we loved to do together was to take to the trails. The running became walking when Stephanie became pregnant and stopped altogether for a while when she gave birth to our two children Jessica and Tyler. However, it was not too long before we were back on the trail with one kid, then two in backpacks or toddling along beside us.

My work took a toll on our getting out. I had had to cancel some of the outings we had planned because there was something due in court, and several times I had arrived home simply too tired. Stephanie still takes the kids out, sometime just to the city park, but occasionally into the woods. Although I enjoy hearing their stories about the birds and animals, and other things they saw, I always wish I could have been with them. I was missing my time in the out-of-doors, but I had recently realized I was also missing out on the life of my family.

One day Stephanie announced she and I were going to spend some time that day out in nature together. We parked the kids with her parents and went for a run on the beach. Falling behind as my energy lagged made me realize I wasn't in the physical shape I wanted to be and, more importantly, not playing the part in the life of my family that I should. We finished our outing together at a quiet restaurant. Looking across the table at the face that had put so much meaning into my life, I knew I had to change the balance of things.

"Stephanie, I think I have been failing to play my part in the family as I should and failing to be there for you. I am thinking maybe I should find a different job, one that would give me more time and energy to do things with you and the kids."

The idea of leaving a job so much a part of who I was made me feel low, but that time with my wife together on the beach reminded me of a part of life I was much less willing to let go of.

"Are you nuts, Steve? Your work as a public defender is part of what our family is, just like my work as a teacher. The fact that we are doing things with so much meaning for us is part of making our family who we are. When you don't make it home in time for bed call, the kids like it when I tell them that you are out bringing justice to poor people. They both can't wait to grow up enough to be able to come and watch you in court.

"The kids and I are going to take some responsibility to drag you away from your work—going to a movie together, watching Jessica at her dance recital, and doing some family camping. The three of us are going to take turns deciding what the four of us should do for fun. And I know your parents or mine will be happy to spend some time with their grandkids while you and I get out and up to speed on the trail again."

I was so happy I cried.

CHAPTER TEN

Jeff Harris Tells His Story

I've been in jail for a month now, awaiting my trial. In comparison with the other jails I've spent time in this one isn't bad. The other guys here are, for the most part, easy to get along with. Those in my unit have all been here before and know how to pass the time. This time around, I find myself one of the older guys, and I don't really know much about what everyone else is talking about. It has given me a chance to think about what has happened in my life so far.

I was born in a small town in Missouri. I had a mom, a dad, and an older brother Bill. We lived in a house that my parents owned. My father had a job at the local factory where they made some sort of car parts that were sold to General Motors. My mother had a part-time job at the Seven Eleven. Those years, until I was about ten, were the best times of my life and I have always hoped Darlene and I, and our two kids, could experience the same comfort.

When I was about ten, the plant shut down. Mom told me later General Motors found a place outside the country to make the parts. Dad changed. He started getting angry all the time and was doing a lot more drinking. He and Mom got into arguments all the time, and there were a couple of times when he slapped her. Once she ended up with a black eye. He couldn't get a job for the longest time. Mom said when he finally got one, he felt really belittled by the simple things he had to do and the way he was treated. One day he just left, and we never saw him again. A few years later, Mom got a petition for divorce from him in the mail from another state, and she signed off on it.

Our family really began to struggle after Dad left. The mortgage payments we could afford when he was there with his good job, we couldn't afford any longer, and we had to sell the house. Mom walked away with nothing from the sale. She had to sell the house for way under what they'd paid for it because of all the vacant houses in town after the plant closed. Mom found herself with a lot of other debts to pay. We moved into a small apartment where my brother Bill and I had to sleep in the living room. Mom looked for a second job, but with the plant closing, jobs were hard to find. The only job she could find was temporary janitorial work where she had to be available at any time and go work at all sorts of different locations. We didn't always have much to eat, and our clothes got pretty old. Mom was tired all the time. She smoked a lot and had a bad cough.

I started to hate school. The other kids taunted me because of my old clothes and the cheap lunches I brought from home. One day, one of my shoes fell apart, and I had to go around the rest of the day with just a sock on one foot. I still remember how the kids laughed at me. There were a couple of guys who were kind of like me—Jack and Fred. We started hanging around together. It was so nice to get to leave behind all the struggles my family was going through and just do crazy things. We started skipping school a lot, and I failed some classes because I wasn't doing the work. I finally stopped going altogether.

Bill was two years ahead of me. The other kids used to taunt him too, but he hung in and graduated. He got married to his girlfriend and moved out. Like Dad, he struggled to find work. He ended up with two jobs involving physical labor and was always so tired every time I saw him. I didn't want to live like that. It was more fun just to be goofing around with Jack and Fred.

The three of us met up with this guy, George. He was older than we were, and he started buying us beer and, before long, crack cocaine. The three of us were always out of money, so George set us up with a deal where we'd steal stuff, and he had people who'd buy it. That worked out pretty well. We'd go steal from stores and give the stuff to George, and he would give us cash. I got to wear new clothes, we could buy all the alcohol and drugs we needed, and we partied at George's, where several girls joined us.

It wasn't long before the three of us got arrested for breaking into a store after hours. We were all seventeen at the time. Jack and Fred were taken to juvenile court, but before the case came to court, I turned eighteen, so I had to go to adult court. I ended up pleading to one count of burglary and spending six months in jail, while Jack and Fred did only ten days in juvie. My mom had been working on me to go back to school, but she got really angry when I ended up in jail.

When I got out of jail, Jack, Fred, and George were waiting. Being at home still wasn't any fun; Mom spent all the time pushing me to go back to school or get a job like Bill. That wasn't for me, so I hooked up with the gang again and we got back to business. George kept pushing us hard for more and more stuff, but the drugs and booze and the girls kept coming, and we were living a carefree life. Sometime when I was nineteen, George asked us to get some guns. Jack and I scouted out the Bass Pro Shop at closing and found they locked up most of the guns but left out the ones in the glass case. We figured a way to hide in the store until it closed, broke into the gun case, and took several guns. We smashed out a window and took off, but the cops caught us in the parking lot, and we were off to jail again.

Jack agreed to tell the police about George and his operation and got to plead guilty to a lesser charge. I wouldn't do that because I knew George had lots of friends working with him both in an out of prison, so I took the full hit, burglary in the first degree, because it was guns we were stealing. I ended up doing 24 months in the prison in Jeff City. I learned a lot in those two years: Do what I am told, whether by the guards or the gang leaders, and stay with those of my race. I also started looking at those "carefree" teenage days a little differently, not just because they ended with me in prison, but I got to thinking there must be something of more value I could be doing with my life. I tried attending Narcotics Anonymous and Alcoholics Anonymous, but I didn't like the religious element, and in those days, I didn't think I was really addicted. It seemed to me my life was getting away, but one day they just let me out on parole. I was twenty-one.

Mom thought I should move out of Missouri to get away from those guys I was with when I got into trouble. I went to live with my brother Bill who had moved to Washington State, had a pretty good job, and was happily living with his wife and kids. I still wasn't ready to settle down. Bill really didn't have a place for me in his house, and I often felt like I was intruding. With my criminal record, work was hard to find. All I could get was temporary jobs. I was staying away from the drugs, but was doing quite a bit of drinking. I needed it to help me relax. Bill was after me to get into treatment; he told Mom, and she came after me as well.

One day, Todd, one of the guys I was working with, invited me to go with him and his girlfriend Rose to the bar after work. We drove in Todd's car, picked up Rose and went to the bar. They were celebrating their decision to get married. Rose had a real job and Todd was going to go to the community college and do some job training. Things got pretty happy. The bartender cut us off, but I had a bottle of Missouri bourbon in my backpack that kept us going. We were all really drunk by the time we were ready to leave. I drove because we thought I was the least intoxicated. Not long after we got underway, I lost control and the car went off the road and hit a tree.

I was knocked out and by the time I regained consciousness, the police and ambulance were there. Todd was dead and Rose was badly hurt. She and I were taken to the hospital, but I was released in a matter of hours. Rose remained in the hospital in critical condition and died two days later. I was taken to jail and charged with two counts of vehicular homicide while under the influence of alcohol. My blood alcohol level was 0.15 percent, well above the 0.08 percent limit. My public defender lawyers tried to help, but they said, with my criminal history, the prosecuting attorney wasn't going to offer any reduction in the charge. Washington State has a detailed formula for deciding how long a sentence will be. With my prior convictions, my sentence range was 51 to 68 months. The judge sentenced me to sixty months, and I was once again off to prison.

I was twenty-four when I went to prison again. Because of my age and the fact my crimes were not intentional violence, I was placed in a unit with fellow inmates older and more at peace with their situation than I had found in Missouri. I finished high school, took some college courses, and worked in prison industries. This time there was no question. I knew I was an alcoholic and became a very regular member of Alcoholics Anonymous. I was happily surprised that the religious element wasn't as predominant as I had found it in Missouri. I think I learned a lot from some of the guys in my unit. There were two guys in particular, Bob and another guy whose name I can't remember. Like me, they had both been in prison before, but they were now in their forties and could see their lives passing away. They were both really committed to getting out and making something positive out of the rest of their lives. They pushed hard on me to do the same, and I have always been grateful to them for that.

My mother died while I was in prison. She got lung cancer, maybe from all that smoking. She couldn't afford some of the treatment options rich people get. Bill was there for her last days. She told him she was so happy he had given her grandchildren, but that her kids were the most important things in her life. That made me angry with myself for having turned out the way I did.

My sentence was sixty months, but with good time I got out after forty when I was twenty-eight. One of the conditions of my sentence was that I do an inpatient alcohol treatment program. Thinking about the two people I killed made me want to do everything I could so "that guy who got away with his life" that night would never touch another drop of alcohol. I did everything they asked me to do, and they made me one of the team leaders.

Darlene came into the program about two weeks after me. She had been in an abusive relationship with a guy and had been doing a lot of drinking to survive. Luckily, her father rescued her from that relationship and brought her to the program, which he paid for with his union health insurance. We were a perfect match, and it was hard to follow the keep-separate rules of the program, but we did. I finished the program ahead of her, but I was waiting at the door when she was discharged.

Darlene's dad wasn't happy to learn about my past, but acting out of nothing but love for his daughter, he came to accept her decision and did come to "give her away" when we got married at the courthouse. He and my brother Bill helped us financially to begin with. Darlene got a job like my mother had, working for a janitorial service, going wherever and whenever she was needed. I could only get temporary jobs to begin with, but I had learned some skills in the prison industries which got me some employment and the Department of Corrections helped me get hooked up with some training in diesel mechanics at the local community college.

Our first child, Jenny, came as a bit of a surprise. We didn't know how we were going to afford another mouth to feed and, more importantly, how the two of us could find time to care for her and still stay working. However, when she arrived, those worries were just overwhelmed by the joy she brought us. We experienced the same joy with Christi's birth four years later. Darlene proved to be a wonderful mother and the most important thing in my life. Every part of family life was a gift from each of us to the other three. However, I couldn't just keep my head inside my family. There was a world out there where Darlene and I had to go to earn enough to keep that family together, rent, food, clothing, and daycare.

On top of everything, there was all the money I owed to the court. When I got sentenced for the vehicular homicides, the judge ordered me to pay what came to twenty thousand dollars. The money was owed to the State of Washington because the state had paid the cost of the funerals for Rose and Todd, for the hospital bills for trying to save Rose, and for some other smaller stuff. Under Washington law, I also owed interest on that debt at a rate of twelve percent. I worked as much as I could in the prison industries and got paid about a dollar an hour. Of that money they took twenty percent to make a payment on what I owed to the state. Another twenty percent went for my room and board in prison, and another ten percent was put into my savings account for when I got out. But all that time, the interest was piling up and by the time I was released I had paid about twelve hundred dollars, and even with those payments my debt to the court had gone up to twenty-seven thousand dollars. I talked to the court clerk just before I got arrested and the guy told me that in the nine years since my release I had increased the total I had paid to forty-seven hundred dollars, but my debt had climbed to over seventy thousand dollars. My brother went on-line and figured out that if I paid the court seven hundred dollars a month, I'd pay off that debt in a hundred years. With that hanging over me, Darlene and I were never going to own a house. We were always going to have to use those prepaid credit cards, and any time we borrowed money, as we did to buy a car so Darlene could get to those places where she worked, we'd have to pay twice the usual interest rate. Our debt was a deep fog that clouded my very existence.

When I got released from prison, there was so much I had to put together to make ends meet for Darlene and me, and Jenny when she came, that the court only ordered me to pay ten dollars a month for the first four years. When I finished my training and got a regular job, the judge upped it to fifty dollars a month. I made every payment until about three months before I was arrested when I lost my job. Kind of like what happened to my dad, the company I was working for lost a contract, and they let me go because I was the most recent mechanic hired. When I couldn't make those payments, I was summoned to court, and the judge told me I needed to pay the next fifty dollars by the following Friday or turn myself in to jail.

Walking out of court that day, I was still determined to make a go of it. I borrowed the fifty dollars from Bill and made an appointment to interview for a job I'd heard about at a diesel mechanics shop. I got the job and was supposed to start that Friday, the same day I would have to report to jail if I hadn't paid the money. My confidence was high when I walked into the court clerk's office to pay the fifty dollars, and it was a huge shock when the money wasn't in my wallet. I went racing home to look for the money. When Darlene told me she had used it to buy shoes and a coat for Christi at the Goodwill, I fell apart. All sorts of things went through my mind: I was going to go to jail; I couldn't take that job; and we couldn't start climbing out of the cellar. The fact that Darlene had used that money to buy clothing for our child reminded me of the time when my shoe fell off when I was a kid. It was the final proof of what a failure I was.

I know I started yelling. No doubt Darlene was walking away because she was a little frightened. When I started to reach for her, she was looking at me, but by the time I got a hold of her she'd turned and was pulling away. I wanted to tell her what a failure I thought I was and was hoping she'd comfort me as she had so many times before. She continued to pull away and started to fall. As she did, I could feel the increased pressure in my hands, and I immediately let her go. She got up and ran out of the house. I thought she would come right back, so I just stayed in the house and was there when the police came. I never tried to strangle her.

CHAPTER ELEVEN

Darlene's Story

Maureen Miller was the investigator assigned for the Harris case. She had been with HCPD for a long time, starting part-time right out of high school. She chose to give us a try because we'd represented her uncle in a theft case that went to trial, and she'd cut class to go to court and watch the proceedings. We weren't able to get an acquittal but were able to get the judge to authorize a work release sentence which allowed the uncle to keep his job and continue to help support his family for the six months of his sentence. Maureen started out with no skills but lots of energy, moving files from here to there as needed. Everyone enjoyed having her around. Along with working with us, she was attending classes at the community college, including classes in criminal justice and the paralegal program. As her skills increased, she took on more responsibilities and a full-time position. When an investigator position opened, she was appointed. In just five years, along with completing her bachelor's degree, Maureen had developed her skills as an investigator and become one of those assigned to more serious cases, including now the Harris case.

Given the mandatory nature of the sentence Jeff was facing, it didn't look like a social worker was going to be of any help at sentencing, but we thought a professional diagnosis could be useful in plea bargaining with the prosecutor. If we hadn't looked, we would never have been sure the insight of a social worker couldn't have been helpful at the trial. Meredith Hayward had assisted me in the Cindy Baker case and in the Gilbert Martin case and had volunteered to see if there was some way she could help with Jeff. With a master's degree in social work, Meredith had come to work at HCPD because she wanted to help people in need. We told her at her interview we had plenty of people in need, but lots of barriers to our efforts to help. Apparently, that was all she needed to hear. She turned down a job with Child Protective Services and began finding ways to help our clients.

—

One day, deep into our investigation of Jeff's case, Maureen and Meredith came into my office. Maureen had told Meredith about Jeff's criminal history, pointing out that those burglaries in his criminal history, including the one that constituted a strike, were committed when he was a teenager. Indeed, Jeff had been seventeen when he committed the second-degree burglary and nineteen when he committed the first-degree burglary, which was his strike number one.

"Can't we use that new science about the juvenile brain to get him a more reasonable sentence," said Meredith. "Miller v. Alabama, the US Supreme court case from a few years ago said that the nature of the teenage brain makes teenagers less culpable for their offenses. How can they count something as a strike for a nineteen-year-old the same as they would count it for someone committing that crime as a thirty-year-old?"

I told Meredith that her reasoning makes perfect sense in the world of science, but the law that came out of the Miller cases wouldn't help us in this case. We weren't facing a sentencing for a teenager. Jeff was 37. Even if we had been, Miller only required consideration of age for teenagers under eighteen.

"But the psychosocial development of the brain," she responded, "doesn't magically catch up with the intellectual development at age eighteen; it takes until a person reaches their late twenties. Statistically, Harris hadn't even reached psychosocial maturity at the time of the vehicular homicides."

"And look what they are doing here," Maureen remarked. "The sentencing significance of this new charge is nothing more than the fact that it is a strike. So, it's no more important in determining Jeff's sentence than the burglary when he was 19 when, maybe not the court, but the science would say he was less culpable. The three-strikes law comes out of the thinking that 'once a bad person, always a bad person.' This science says that's BS and the way Jeff has worked to turn his life around confirms the science."

Meredith and Maureen were right; the problem was to find some way to bring that into court. I had been doing some thinking about the sentencing if Jeff got convicted. It was looking like all I would be able to do is stand there like an idiot. I had to find something to present to the court, and the arguments Maureen and Meredith were making seemed like the best place to begin.

With some relief in my heart, I gave Meredith the OK to prepare a report to the court arguing for Jeff's diminished responsibility for those burglaries, particularly that first degree burglary. I told Meredith that Maureen had a complete biography of Jeff and could fill her in on the particular psychosocial disabilities Jeff was living with when he was seventeen and nineteen and committed those burglaries, but the two of them were ahead of me and that had already been done.

Meredith began to outline the argument they were preparing. She noted that Jeff's family fell apart just about the time he became a teenager, when statistics show that psychosocial maturity declines. Young people become less likely to consider the future consequences of their actions, have poor impulse control, and become vulnerable to pressure from others. Jeff's decisions to quit school, to spend his time with those other uncontrolled teenagers—Jack and Fred, and to start committing thefts and burglaries under George's direction were made with a brain that did not have the same powers of thought an adult would have used. Maureen pointed out that it was equally significant that Jeff had turned things around so well. He had committed himself to a better life while in prison and, when released, had settled down with a family and a profession. And he had had no criminal arrests for nine years. All proved that he had achieved psychosocial maturity and those burglaries were no longer part of who he was and shouldn't count as a strike.

"Meredith, I am not sure how it will help Jeff's case, but it is certainly something we will want to have in the tool kit."

—

Maureen was able to get in touch with Darlene and schedule a time for an interview. Because she could no longer pay the rent, Darlene and her children had moved into her father's apartment. It worked best for her to do the interview there. Darlene answered the door and invited the two of us in. She was a good match for her husband, tall and pretty, with long brown hair. The apartment wasn't very large. There were two bedrooms. Darlene's father kept his and she slept on an air mattress in the other one, which her father used as an office and where he kept his computer. Jenny and Christi slept in the living room, alternating on the couch and another air mattress. We conducted the interview in the living room, which was efficiently organized to serve both its functions. Christi was playing on the floor. During our interview, she came up to her mother and, after receiving an encouraging word and a pat on the shoulder returned to her play. Darlene told us Jenny was at school but would be home before long.

Maureen decided to get some family background before focusing in on the incident. Darlene told us she'd grown up in a home with her mother and father until they divorced. She then lived with her mother with alternate weekends and some holidays with her father. Her mother became an alcoholic, and she joined in when she became eighteen. They survived together somehow for the next two years, and Darlene did manage to graduate from high school, but all that time had been pretty much a blur. She had had several boyfriends and got pregnant once but had a miscarriage. Her father kept after her mother and her to get into treatment. Somewhere during that time, he landed a good job, and his union contract had a provision that would pay for her inpatient treatment. Darlene went just to please her father, and that was where she met Jeff.

"Darlene, has your mother gotten into treatment?" inquired Maureen.

"No, she hasn't. My dad and I have been after her to get help, but because they are divorced, she couldn't qualify under his policy, and she hasn't really wanted to get help. We are still hoping she will."

"So, it was in treatment where you met Jeff?" I asked.

"Yes, and although the counsellors were helping me learn things I needed to turn my life around, Jeff's commitment to his sobriety helped me—and a lot of the others in the program—to commit to ours. The two of us developed a relationship while in treatment, and the counselors had to work overtime to keep us focused on the steps in our treatment. Jeff completed the program before I did and, by the rules, we couldn't communicate while I finished, but he was there when I was discharged, and I had to choose between him and my dad for my ride home.

"When my dad learned Jeff had a criminal record, he was staunchly opposed to our continuing relationship, but I insisted.

The two of them always talked about things when Jeff came to pick me up, and one night, when I came home from a date, Dad told me he thought Jeff was a smart and highly motivated guy, and he was happy I had found someone so nice. Not long after that, Jeff and I decided to get married.

"Jeff has made me very happy. I so enjoy those times when we sit together and talk."

"What kind of things do you like to talk about?" inquired Maureen.

"You know, it's not so much what we talk about; it's just being together and talking about something that matters to one of us that makes me happy."

"I can see you enjoy Christi's company too," I commented.

"Our kids are a really important part of our family. Jeff is a good father; he loves them so much and they miss him a lot.

"I love being married and having a family, but the downside is we have had to struggle so hard to pay for what we have, and our wish list just keeps growing without any hope. Jeff and I each finished treatment with almost nothing. I did graduate from high school but had no job training. With taking care of the kids and needing to do something to bring in money right now, I haven't been able to do any job training, so I work part time for a janitorial company. Jeff got some training in prison and took some classes in diesel mechanics but struggled to get a good job because of his record. With Jeff in jail, we had to leave our apartment and move in here with my dad. With Jeff gone, I have to turn down jobs to take care of the kids unless Dad is home from work or Mary, our neighbor where we used to live, was available."

"Do you have medical insurance?" Maureen asked.

"No, we don't. I've had to take the kids to the emergency room a couple of times. Once Jenny broke her arm falling off a slide in the playground. We got all the medical services we needed and Jenny's alright now, but we ended up with a very large bill that still hasn't been paid.

"There is another thing that has us going crazy now. The lady with the prosecutor's office."

"Their witness advocate?"

"Yes, she called in the Child Protective Services, and they sent Mrs. Sinclair to come and inspect us. Mrs. Sinclair said she was considering taking our family into court. She told me Jenny and Christi had to get better clothes and it was harmful for them to be living in these close quarters with my dad. Mrs. Sinclair wouldn't believe Jeff didn't break Jenny's arm until I showed her the letter from the school, and we had to get a letter from the teacher to show her that Jenny was doing well in her classes. The last thing she said to us was that things were OK now with Jeff in jail, but if he gets released, she will take us to court. Because Jeff has those criminal convictions, she just puts him in the box with all the other people with felony records and will not believe that he hasn't been physically and mentally abusing me and that he has been a good father to our kids."

It was time to talk about the incident. Darlene took Christi into her father's bedroom, along with a few of her toys, and turned on the television. It wasn't long into our discussion that Jenny came home from school and Darlene sent her in to her father's bedroom to play and watch television with her sister.

For the most part Darlene's description matched Jeff's. She did take money out of Jeff's wallet to buy a coat and shoes for Christi. She didn't know that money had a special purpose and apparently it was not unusual for her to go to Jeff's wallet when a family need arose. Jeff would go into her purse too when he had to pay for a family need. She had been totally shocked when he started yelling because that wasn't like him at all. She'd stepped back to get some distance and, as he grabbed for her, she turned and started to walk away, at which point she tripped and started to fall. Jeff let go at that point, but he was still yelling at her, so she ran out of the house to her neighbor's.

"Darlene," Maureen asked, "I want to look closely at the time when Jeff had his hands around your neck; is that a part of a special way you communicate.?"

"No, that is the first time he had ever held me that way. It really surprised me; it is one of the things that got me so frightened."

"I need you to give me a moment-to-moment description of what happened during the time Jeff's hands were around your neck."

"When he first grabbed me, I was facing him; I started to back up and turned around and tried to get out of his grip. I was trying to get away and I felt his grip get tighter. I started choking and about the same time I fell, and Jeff let me go."

"Can you tell us anything more about what you meant when you said you started choking?" I asked, hoping she would say something we could use for the defense.

"There were a couple of moments when I couldn't get my breath."

That answer had us dead to rights on half of what the prosecutor would have to prove.

"Darlene," continued Maureen, "was the pressure of Jeff's hands spread evenly around your neck?"

"I can't be sure but, thinking about it now, I am mostly remembering the pressure away from him. So, when I was backing away from him, it was on the back of my neck and when I turned around, it was at the front."

Maureen's interrogation had given us a much clearer picture of where we stood for trial. Darlene was going to tell the jury her breath was restricted, but she was also going to give us some wiggle room as to whether that was something Jeff intended.

We had learned a lot from Darlene, and it was getting to be time to leave when her father arrived home.

"Dad, this is Jeff's lawyer Mr. Cole and the investigator Ms.

Miller. This is my father, Michael Houser."

"Darlene told me you were going to be here today, and I was hoping to get home from work to meet you and tell you what I think."

"I am glad we were still here, Mr. Houser," responded Maureen. "We definitely want to know what you think about Jeff's case, but can we start by having you tell us a little bit about yourself?"

"Please call me Mike. I started out in the Army, stationed at several bases in the United States, and did see combat in Iraq. I ended my service at Fort Lewis before they changed the name to Joint Base Lewis-McCord. Darlene was born when I was stationed at Fort Leonard Wood in Missouri. We found out later Jeff was born in Missouri too. After I left the service, it took me quite a while to get a good job, but now I am a member of the International Brotherhood of Electrical Workers, solving people's electrical problems around here.

"Darlene's mother, Janet, and I were married for 20 years. I dragged her around the country to the places where I was stationed. In the end, it didn't work out, and we got a divorce. A lot of that was my fault. I came back from Iraq with a lot of stress from my time in combat. A guy right next to me got shot in the head and died on the spot, and ever since, I couldn't stop thinking about why it was him instead of me. It changed who I was, and that was not the guy she'd married. We both walked away in a lot of trouble, but I got help from the military.

"I wanted to tell you what I thought of Jeff and offer to help in any way I could. Darlene has probably told you when I first heard she was dating an ex-con, I was all over her to break it up. She wouldn't hear of it and they kept dating. I saw him when he came over to pick her up. He and I started talking. It was pretty negative from my side to begin with, but Jeff met all my questions with real answers. His life's mistakes were bigger than mine, but I have certainly had some of my own and if I'm going to allow myself to start over, I need to allow Jeff to do the same, especially, after he had paid such a price. I wasn't there when this thing happened, but I know from what I have experienced about Jeff and his relationship with Darlene that what happened was an accident."

"Thank you, Mike," I replied. "I will keep that in mind as we continue to prepare."

While we were talking to Mike, Darlene had gone into the bedroom, collected her daughters, and brought them out to meet us. They were polite and comfortable in the company of their mother and grandfather. The girls introduced themselves and told us their ages: Jenny, age 8 and Christi, age 3. They told us they loved their dad and wanted him to come home soon to play with them. Jenny wanted to show him an essay she had written on which she got an A.

By this time, we had everything we thought we needed and a lot more, so it was time to leave. Maureen and I got into the car and headed back to the office. Maureen started the conversation.

"Interviews like this one always get me to question again the general picture I keep in my head about our clients. Most of my work as an investigator involves interviews of angry victims, righteous cops, and clients in denial. I walk away from those interviews thinking of our clients solely in terms of what they did, or did not do, and measuring our work as a scoreboard of wins and losses. But then you do an investigation like this one and get to see the client in the broader dimensions of that person's life. My first thought is this guy must be an exception to the rule, but then, on second thought, maybe a lot of the rest of these guys have another dimension in their lives too that we didn't have time to look at. And if we did take the time to look more closely, they might look more human too."

Maureen was right, and I acknowledged my agreement, but my thoughts were headed in a different, and more personal direction. I spent the rest of the drive silently navigating through them. I consider myself to be quite successful. I have a wife and two kids, like Jeff. But my wife is fully employed as a fourth-grade teacher, my kids dress in new clothes and go to professional childcare when not in school, and we own our home. Neither of our salaries are what we would like, and we have a big mortgage and considerable student debt, but we do have enough income to take care of our needs, make reasonable payments against our debts, save for the future, and get to do some fun things now and again. I was thinking about all of that as I drove because I know there is some part of me that feels I deserve what I have. I studied hard all the way through school and worked summers during college and law school. But talking to Darlene and her father and meeting Jeff's kids has me questioning my sense of entitlement. They were smart too, worked hard and are totally committed to doing the right thing and yet have done nothing but struggle. I was borne into a well-functioning family with plenty of resources to provide for all my needs and many of my wants, including a large part of the cost of my education. If all those advantages were taken away, and my parents and I had to confront all the roadblocks Darlene has had to confront, where would I be now? I decided it is more of "good fortune" and less of "what I deserve" that has me where I am.

CHAPTER TWELVE
Hat in Hand

With our interview of Darlene Harris completed, the next step was to see what kind of plea offer we can get from the prosecutor's office. So, I arranged a meeting with the prosecutor Bob Winston. If not done in the courtroom or in an email exchange, plea negotiations are almost always held in the prosecutor's office, probably because we are usually the ones with our hats in our hands, and that was certainly true in this case. I was feeling a little more empowered than usual negotiating this case. It seemed so obvious that a life sentence for what happened here would be an incredible injustice.

Winston had the prosecutor's file for the Harris case open on his desk when I arrived. He also had the social workers report Meredith had prepared.

"Steve, I have been reviewing the evidence in this case and I don't see any problems for us if we go to trial."

"Bob, it's not the evidence I want to talk about, it's the potential consequences of a conviction. First of all, if there was a strangulation in this case, it was not the sort of thing the legislature had in mind when they made strangulation a per se second-degree assault. Whatever it was that occurred at the time, it was not something that had ever happened between the Harrises before, and, although Ms. Harris was frightened, she suffered no injury as a result. A life sentence is totally out of proportion with what happened."

"It's not just what happened here that puts your client in this position. It's more about his criminal history, two burglaries, one of them a burg one, and two homicides."

"But he was seventeen and nineteen when those burglaries were committed and the burg one involved only a theft of firearms, not the use of a firearm. And those two 'vehicular' homicides occurred in a single incident when he was only 24. That social worker report we gave you makes it clear those burglaries and even the vehicular homicides were committed when Harris' brain had not yet matured. He is now 37 and has been out of prison for nine years without any criminal behavior. He's gotten married, has two kids, and is a trained diesel mechanic. It's this stupid three-strikes law.

"Steve, stupid or not, it's a law. And whether you like it or not, it is the law in Washington."

It occurred to me to respond that only increased the scope of its stupidity, but I was there to get a better deal for Jeff and not to engage in a political argument, so I went in a different direction.

"Bob, the only way the three-strikes law can be made to work is if prosecutors exercise discretion in deciding when to use it."

"You are right about that, and my supervisor and I have been talking with our administration to figure out what kind of offer to make to you. You will hear from me tomorrow."

I walked away with some hope. I have had good luck negotiating with Winston. Unlike some other prosecutors who saw themselves as soldiers for "the good" against "the evil," Winston had always been willing to consider the cases he handled from all perspectives. However, I knew from talking to him that Jeff's case had some political ramifications, and their plea offer would be made by the higher-ups.

—

The next day came and when I arrived at the office after an early morning visit to the jail, I saw the text message to call Winston. Anxious to get the news, I immediately called back, but he wasn't by his phone, so I just had to leave a message for him with my office and cellphone numbers, and Polly's number just in case. An hour of tension further into the day, Winston caught me.

"Steve, here is the offer, and it's the only offer you are going to get. Mr. Harris pleads guilty to solicitation to commit a second-degree assault, which is not a strike. He will have to state he did strangle his wife and agree to the high end of the range which, for him, is 42 and three quarters months in prison."

That still seemed to me to be an awfully stiff sentence for what happened here, but I agreed to get Winston a response as soon as I could get over to see Jeff. Polly managed to get the jail to give me time with Jeff that afternoon. I walked over to the jail and into the interview room thinking I had good news. The prosecutor's offer would have Jeff spending a long time in prison, but with the good time which he was sure to earn, he would do 28 and a half months in prison, which would have him out of prison before he turned forty. Jeff came in and sat down, and I relayed to him the prosecutor's offer.

It wasn't good news to Jeff; he sat back in his chair, looked up, and said nothing.

"Jeff, we are dealing with a pretty terrible law, and we don't have much bargaining power. The prosecutor in your case has been talking to the higher-ups in his office and this is the only offer they are going to make. Unless you take this deal, we will have to go to trial, and if we don't win the trial, you would spend the rest of your life in prison."

"But I didn't choke her. I am not going to plead to that offer."

"Jeff, I have looked at this case from every angle and all of my experience in criminal law supports my recommendation that you take the prosecutor's offer."

"Mr. Cole, there is another angle outside of your legal experience... and that's what I can live with. I'm not taking the deal."

I asked Jeff to give himself 24 hours. I told him to call his brother Bill and get his opinion. Because he wasn't allowed to talk to her, I said I would call Darlene and get a message from her.

"If you are going to take the risk of trial, you are going to have to do it knowing what the two adults that love you think."

Jeff took a deep breath and after a short pause said OK. He was to call me at the office in the morning and I'd tell him what Darlene had to say and would be over to see him in the afternoon for a further discussion. I signaled the guards that we were done, gathered my papers, and when the guards took Jeff away, I headed quickly back to the office to call Bill and Darlene.

—

I was able to get hold of Bill and explain the offer and what was at stake. He wanted a numerical percentage of Jeff's chances at trial. I told him I couldn't give him that, but I thought the chances of a conviction were high. I asked Bill just to listen to Jeff when he called and give him an honest response to what he says. The call to Darlene was more difficult. She didn't want the case to go to trial where she would be compelled to testify against a husband she loved, but she also didn't want to push that agenda against whatever decision Jeff felt was right. In the end, her message to Jeff was that she loved him and would wait for him to get out after serving his sentence, but he should do what his heart tells him to do.

Jeff did call the next morning and I told him what Darlene

had said. He told me Bill had urged him to take the deal and had promised to help Darlene and his daughters while he was in prison. Jeff wanted to talk further on the phone, but I told him we needed to do this face to face. I had scheduled time in the afternoon and right after lunch, I headed over to the jail.

I started our conversation, reiterating that a conviction for second-degree assault would mean a sentence of life in prison. There would be no parole board that would come along and let him out, and at age thirty-seven, he would probably spend forty years or more in prison. Accepting the plea deal would have him out before turning 40 and he would have 40 or more years of freedom.

"If we go to trial, the prosecutor is going to have to convince the jury 'beyond a reasonable doubt' that when you put your hands around Darlene's neck you intended to restrict her breathing or the blood flow to the brain. To prove that, it is undisputed you came home angry because Darlene had used the money you needed to pay the court. You've admitted you grabbed her around the neck. And Darlene has been clear: there was a time when your hands were around her neck and her breathing was restricted.

"Jeff, as bad as it will be to have to spend twenty-eight and a half months in prison, the risk of a life sentence is too great, and I strongly recommend you take the deal."

"Mr. Cole, I appreciate how you have handled this. I have considered all the legal angles you have presented, and I was glad I had a chance to talk to my brother and to know what Darlene is thinking. I still want to go to trial and try for an acquittal. I didn't strangle Darlene and I am never going to say I did.

"But that is not the only reason for my decision. Ever since I got out of prison, I have been struggling to live a good life. I don't mean just being a good person; in addition to being a good person, I wanted to be able to get the benefits of being a good person. I have had three wonderful benefits, Darlene, and our two girls,

Jenny and Christi. But everything else I have been involved with has been a struggle, much of it because I am a convicted felon. I have been turned down for jobs when the employer learns I have a record. We've been turned down for apartments, and when the word got out in my neighborhood that I had a record, not all, but some of our neighbors, including the parents of Jenny's best friend, became somewhat standoffish.

"The fact I have a wife and kids, although the most important things in my life, actually makes my life more difficult because they deserve so much more than I can give them. Darlene would be able to get a far better job if she had the time and the money to get some training. Jenny is doing really well in school, but neither she nor Christi have ever had new clothes to wear. They've had to rely completely on the free breakfast and lunch at school, and we haven't been able to afford the dance classes for Jenny that all her friends are in. We have always planned for the kids to go to college, but we haven't been able to put anything aside to help pay for it."

"But isn't it better for you to be able to start working on those projects in a little over two years than not be able to help at all?"

"No, because I can't just set the clock ahead two years. I'm going to be older with less time to build a life, my kids are going to be older with greater needs, and Darlene will be putting her life on hold, waiting for me to get out. When I got that job just before I got arrested, I thought of it as my last chance to build the life I wanted; there were so many things I wanted to accomplish, I knew I had to get going. I can't wait two more years.

"My debt to the court is another reason for my decision. When I was sentenced for the vehicular homicides, the judge imposed $20,000 restitution. I have managed to pay $4,700, but at the 12 percent interest rate set by Washington law, my debt to the court is now over $70,000. If I go away for another two years, that debt will be over $90,000. And that debt I currently share with my wife and kids who are in no way responsible for it but suffer fully from its existence."

I told Jeff, Washington law did allow him to come back to the court and get release from the interest when he had paid off the twenty thousand dollars. But he had been doing the math.

"If I start paying the $50 a month the court has been ordering, when I get out at about age forty, it will take me twenty-five years to pay what is remaining of the twenty thousand. I will be sixty-five and my kids will be thirty-five and thirty and long gone. And Darlene and I still would not have been able to buy a house or do anything else on credit."

"But Jeff, that burden is going to follow you and your family regardless of your decision about the plea offer."

"You are right. That debt will follow me regardless of what I decide to do. If I go to trial and win, that is a fight Darlene and I will take on. If I lose, I am going to file for a divorce and that debt and its consequences will become mine alone and the State of Washington can take the twenty cents out of every dollar-an-hour I earn for the rest of my life. I still want to win the trial, but sometimes I think I ought to just plead guilty to the third strike and get the State of Washington to pay my room and board for the rest of my life.

"I've been to prison twice; I know how to play the game there and it doesn't frighten me. I'll be able to spend my time helping others and maybe I'll write a book, or a bunch of books. All the while, I will know Darlene and the girls are not saddled with that ridiculous debt and all the negatives of an association with a convicted felon. I know Darlene and her father will be able to start something going, and I think there is every chance there will be another guy for her that can give her a better life than I could if I walk out of jail today. No, I am going to fight this case and hope upon hope I win, but I am not going to give in to the prosecutor's plea offer."

I had no answer for that. It did occur to me Jeff's projected debt was not that large in comparison to the debts some of my lawyer colleagues had built getting through law school, but while their debts were a tool for building a career that would give them the life they wanted, Jeff's debt was just a punch in the face that stood as a barrier to everything in life he wanted. His bitterness was perfectly understandable. I walked back from the jail thinking I had to make another try to get a better plea offer from the prosecutor. A misdemeanor assault with a couple of months in jail would certainly be something Jeff would accept. Back at the office, I called Winston, who said he was going to try to arrange a meeting for me the next day with the Hudson County Prosecutor.

—

Bradley Cantrell is the elected Prosecuting Attorney for Hudson County. Winston was able to get me an appointment with him and his Chief Criminal Deputy, Pamela Berens. Winston was there as well. I had often negotiated cases with Berens, but my only prior contact with Mr. Cantrell was a handshake during the last election where he won re-election unopposed. Once the county's political mechanism settles on a candidate, and the county and city police unions get on board, there is never any real contest for election of the Prosecutor.

"Mr. Cantrell, I am Steven Cole, and I am representing Jeff Harris. Thank you for letting me talk to you and Ms. Berens about this case."

"Steve, it's good to see you again. You public defenders play an important part of the criminal justice system in Hudson County. Bob has filled us in on your case, and he and Pamela and I have been talking about it."

Although I could see he had the license to be informal, I didn't think I did.

"Mr. Cantrell, and Ms. Berens, sending Jeff Harris to prison for what happened in this case would be a complete injustice. I'm asking you to allow him to plead guilty to fourth-degree assault and do another two months in jail. Jeff needs to get back to supporting his family. This is not just what he wants, it's what his wife, the victim, and their two kids want and desperately need. The physical contact between Jeff and Darlene--"

"Who is Darlene?" Cantrell interjected.

"That's the victim, Harris' wife." Winston answered.

"Yes," I continued. "The physical contact between Jeff and Darlene was not the sort of thing the legislature had in mind when they made strangulation a version of assault two. There was absolutely no resulting injury here."

"But Steve," responded Berens, "this case isn't just about the assault, it's a three-strikes case, and your client should be going to prison for the rest of his life, but we have considered that and are offering you a way out. Your guy's criminal history is way too serious to give him a misdemeanor. Solicitation to assault two is as good as it's going to get."

I was losing badly and was thinking about attacking the three-strikes law, but Cantrell spoke next.

"I can appreciate the three-strikes law can have some harsh consequences. But as the Hudson County Prosecutor, I have always kept in mind what John Adams said: 'We are a nation of laws, not of men.' And whether I agreed with the goal of the law or liked what happened when it was applied to a particular situation, I took it as my duty to enforce that law. That's where I am with the three-strikes law. If your client gets convicted on his third strike, he should spend the rest of his life in prison and I can't consider how good a person he may be or how it would affect his wife and children, and that's because it's what the law says. It's Mr. Harris' criminal history that makes this a three-strikes case, but we have made you an offer to avoid a life sentence. It would be an affront to the three-strikes law if we offered you anything less."

I wanted to respond but couldn't think of anything that could counter their reasoning when they will always start from the premise that "it's the law and not the people that must be served." Being a nation of laws was supposed to be a protection against a dictator that would rule uncontrolled by the laws the rest of us had to follow. However, a consequence of sanctifying the law to accomplish that purpose leaves instances of great injustice for a significant number of the men and women of this nation, now including Jeff.

"Well, Bob, it looks like we have a trial. We will be ready on the current trial date."

I expressed my appreciation to Mr. Cantrell and Ms. Berens for agreeing to meet and headed back to my office. On the way, it occurred to me these prosecutors had complete control over what kind of game we were about to play, but nothing to really lose if we managed to win. For Jeff, his whole life was on the line.

CHAPTER THIRTEEN
What Syndey Had to Say

My anxiety about Jeff's case took me in to see Sydney. He has always looked at things a little differently, and I was hoping he'd help me find a way to think differently and gain some perspective on what I was doing. Sydney was known in the office for being a little long winded. I think he got it from his father who had been a Lutheran minister. But he was the most experienced lawyer in our office, and it always seemed that what he had to say was well thought out.

The first thing you notice walking into his office is stacks of files all over the floor, a long dead bonsai plant in one corner that had been given to him by the mother of a client where he had won an acquittal, and the coat he had most recently warn thrown over a chair. In court, he's always fully prepared and effective, but it is a mystery to the rest of us at HCPD how he can be so competent given the organizational disaster that is his office. The other thing unique about his office is the plaque on the wall with a quote from the movie *Animal House,* a statement made by Otter just after all the members of Delta house were expelled from Faber College by Dean Wermer: "This Situation Absolutely Requires a Really Stupid and Futile Gesture." I went to see him because I was feeling that the Harris case was one of those "situations" and I didn't know what kind of "gesture" to make.

I told Sydney about Jeff's decision to turn down a plea offer to a reduced charge and go to trial on what would be his third strike.

"Sydney, part of my frustration is not being able to get Jeff to take the plea offer. I've had lots of clients refuse their plea deals and I remained comfortable with the consequences because if the client got convicted, the sentence seemed to be a not totally unreasonable punishment. This case is different because we are headed for a life sentence which would be so unfair. It would be unfair even if Jeff changes his mind and accepts the plea offer because he would be giving up his right to contest the charges under the threat of the life sentence."

As usual Sydney had a lot to say. He began telling me about the three-strikes law. It was a State initiative passed by a 75 percent favorable vote of the people and came at a time when such legislation was highly favored all over the nation. Although not as draconian as Washington's version, many other states had adopted three-strikes laws, and a federal version was enacted in the strongly supported 1994 crime bill. Once it made it to the ballot, the extreme penalty it called for was justified to the voter by tales in the media of extremely violent crimes.

"The problem," said Sydney, "was that the way the law was constructed, it would not be limited to the worst of the worse, but to a lot of others in the process, including possibly your client."

He told me about a client he had represented twenty-five years ago, whose three strikes were all robberies where no one was hurt, and his total take from the three robberies was about five hundred dollars and the client was still in prison, serving a life sentence at a cost to those tax paying voters of $112.96 a day.[2]

---

[2] In 2021 the Washington State Legislature passed a law that allowed for resentencing eliminating second degree robbery as a strike in calculating the score for a new sentence. Sydney's client would be released, but not before he had served 21 times the maximum standard range sentence under the new law.

"You know, Steve, it's not just the voters who failed here. Our legislature, with all the resources necessary to find a proper balance between the weight of the crimes and the weight of the punishments has failed. Although finally, after 26 years, they did eliminate second-degree robbery as one of the strike crimes, they have been unwilling to fully correct the voters—the ones who keep re-electing them—with any fundamental changes to the law. And the state courts have failed us too; against many challenges, they continued to find the law to be not unconstitutionally cruel."

"Sydney, you are not helping me. I have always respected the law, and that respect has provided me with some comfort in the cases I lost. Here, you have given me reasons to disrespect the law that has control of a case I am a part of, and as the defense attorney I may be one of the agents in doing a very bad thing."

Sydney provided me with a different perspective on the law.

"It's not just the three-strikes law. Even the best laws suffer from the same intrinsic ineptitude. There will always be exceptions to the general good a law is intended to achieve where something bad results. Applying the sentence the law prescribes for the burglary that would be appropriate for the person who breaks down the front door of a home, steals the computer and television, and destroys family heirlooms would be an injustice for the homeless person who enters a home through an unlocked front door and takes a sandwich out of the refrigerator."

"But I'm probably going to get a plea bargain for the homeless guy."

"True, we can make the law look a little better because prosecutors have discretion in what they charge and the plea bargains they offer, and judges have some discretion in the sentences they impose. And all those ways that the law can be rescued should be telling us that law is not the final truth. Instead, we look past the circumstances of a particular situation and let the law define what is the good and the bad. A burglary is bad because it fits the definition of burglary regardless of the harm done. Our society needs laws, but we need to see their frailty and apply it, not as a commandment, but as the fallible tool it is."

"So, if it isn't the law, what master am I serving?"

"Steve, you know the answer to that; first and foremost, we represent the client."

"But Sydney, where does that obligation come from. It sounds a bit like what Polly was talking about when she said we were doing what Mother Teresa's Sisters were doing on the streets of Calcutta, but I didn't think many of us would be doing what we were doing under a commandment from God."

"You are right there, but I don't think we have to reach out that far. The Declaration of Independence tells us that 'all men are created equal' with those 'unalienable rights' to 'life, liberty, and the pursuit of happiness.'"

"Yeah, but how does that help us here?"

"Well, while everybody can see the Declaration of Independence as validating their own claim of those rights, if you think about it, it also imposes a duty on us, ignored by far too many, to protect those rights we cling to so strongly for ourselves for all the other 'men' as well."

"But, in situations like I have with Jeff, doesn't that put me at odds with the law?"

"Yes, it does, and that just shows that we are fundamentally at odds with the other players in the legal system whose first duty is to the law."

It occurred to me there was some kind of truth in what Sydney was saying. My conversations with the prosecutors when I went to negotiate about Jeff's case was certainly a demonstration that their thoughts were not about the person we were talking about, but first and foremost about serving the law. Judges too, although they have a lot of discretion in what they do, are ultimately bound by the law whether they like it or not. But even if I am not a soldier of the law, my role in Jeff's case was probably going to facilitate what this lousy law has in store.

There is an ethics rule for attorneys that permits a lawyer to withdraw from a case where the client insists on doing something the lawyer "considers repugnant or with which the lawyer has a fundamental disagreement."

"Sydney, why can't I just withdraw from Jeff's case. I certainly have a fundamental disagreement with his decision not to accept the plea offer."

"The problem is," responded Sydney, "Mr. Harris has the right to go to trial and the right to be represented by counsel at that trial. A privately hired attorney might be able to withdraw from a case they didn't like, but that ethics rule doesn't work for an attorney who is a public defender. If you withdrew from the case, we'd just have to replace you with one of your colleagues, and they'd end up in the same predicament you are in."

I didn't really want to withdraw from Jeff's case. I had developed a great deal of respect for him. He was smart, devoted to his family, and committed to doing what he thought was the right thing. I wanted to do everything I could for him. That was one of the reasons I was so frustrated. This was definitely one of those "situations' where I could use some of the wisdom from the *Animal House* plaque. But I had seen that plaque in Sydney's office for years and it always seemed to me that doing anything "stupid and futile" would only get me kicked off the case, while another lawyer was put in my place to do what I had refused to do, and I'd be disciplined by the state bar.

"So, Sydney, I am not seeing how your *Animal House* plaque is going to be of any help here. There is no homecoming parade to disrupt or a Dean Wermer to foil. The law isn't going to let me get away with something like that."

"You're right, Steve. The plaque isn't giving us permission to disobey the law. What it does tell us, though, is that we cannot be solely motivated in our work simply to bring about what the law requires. We have an overriding challenge of service to the client. In that regard our job in the court system is different from that of prosecutors and judges. I take Otter's message to be that there are times when our commitment to the interest of our client takes us into a situation that is really stupid and futile, and we shouldn't try to make ourselves think it is anything else."

This conversation with Sydney didn't leave me with a clear picture of what to do next, but it certainly gave me some things to think about. We had talked for quite a while, and it had gotten late. I needed to get home to spend the evening with my family as I had promised them and get to work early the next morning to give myself some more time with Jeff.

As I walked down the hall, Laura Berg called out from in her office.

"Did Sydney give you one of his talks about his *Animal House* plaque?"

"Sure did."

"What did you think?"

"You know, I think he has something. I'm hoping it's going to make me a little more at peace doing what I have to do."

I did get a better night's sleep. For the first time in a week, two a.m. came and went without me being aware of it. I was not sure the extra sleep was the result of the talk with Sydney or a good evening with Stephanie, Tyler, and Jessica. But you know, it may have been the talk with Sydney that sent me home with a little more peace of mind, which led to a better time with my family.

—

The first thing on my list the next morning was another trip to see Jeff.

"Jeff, I have been struggling with your decision to go to trial, but I want you to know I am a hundred percent behind you on this. It has been difficult for me to accept your decision because I couldn't help but see things in the context I was used to. But then I haven't lived the life you have, and it has taken me a while, but I have learned a lot about you and have a better understanding of why you are doing what you are doing."

"Mr. Cole, things were a little rough between us to begin with. It was so frustrating for me to find myself back in custody again after so many years of me doing things right. I so wanted to get back out to be with my family. I've pled guilty every time I have been in court and, looking back, I don't see I had any alternatives, but this time I really didn't want to go that way. I know most of what you did in preparation for my case was done in your office, at the court, in the investigation, and talking to the prosecutor, but all those times you did visit helped me understand what was going on and has given me real confidence I am going to get the best possible defense."

Jeff had been well prepared for his part in the trial. I spent some time at this meeting describing how things were going to go when we got to the courtroom as the case proceeded through the trial, hoping to reduce his anxiety, which would in turn, reduce mine. I decided I was overstaying my welcome when he had answered "no, I understand" three times in a row, and I realized his anxiety was under better control than mine. We shook hands, and I went back to the office to get help from other lawyers with some hearings scheduled in my other cases, so I could fully concentrate on Jeff's trial.

CHAPTER FOURTEEN
The Trial

The day of trial arrived. It was going to be a simple case, no expert testimony from scientists or psychologists and no more than six witnesses, which meant the case would only last two or three days. However, there was so much riding on it for Jeff, and his family. For me, it was going to be a test of my ability to work within the confines of a law I felt was wrong in so many ways.

We had been assigned to the court of Judge Jennifer Tibbits. As with several of our judges, she had been a prosecutor before becoming a judge; however, she knew the law and applied it fairly. She was a careful judge, so she was a good draw for our side, which left me haunted only by what the jury would decide.

The trial was scheduled to start at nine o'clock in the morning. Winston and I arrived at the door of the courtroom at about the same time.

"Jeff, your client is walking into a life sentence. Our offer is still open; Harris pleads to solicitation to commit assault two and we agree to the high end of the standard range."

"Thanks, Bob, but we need to go to trial on this."

Inside the courtroom, the two of us went to our assigned tables and went about arranging our respective paperwork. After a short wait, the jail guards brought Jeff in, his handcuffs were removed, and he sat down beside me.

"Jeff, I know what your decision is, and I am not going to say any more about it, but the law requires me to tell you the prosecutor's offer is still open." Jeff looked straight ahead and didn't say a thing, but I knew what he was telling me.

The court staff entered and took their seats. "All rise," said the judge's law clerk. Everyone stood and Judge Tibbits entered in her black robe and took her seat on the bench.

The first order of business was motions in limine. Winston asked the court to prevent us from asking Darlene what she wanted to happen. I knew that motion was going to be granted. Whether to prosecute a case is a decision for the prosecuting attorney; that is why "prosecutor" is an elective office in this state, as it is most other states.

Nevertheless "Your Honor, I object. We are trying to do justice here, and there is no justice when the people most involved don't have a say."

"Your Honor, our office has had a long conversation with Ms. Harris. We know she doesn't want her husband convicted of this crime. We've given that a lot of consideration and have decided to proceed with this case. It's not her call; it's our call to charge the crime, and it will be up to the jury to decide on a verdict."

I couldn't help myself. "It will be up to a jury, but a jury completely blind to the consequences of their decision."

The judge did what I was afraid of.

"Mr. Cole, Mr. Winston is right. I am ordering that Ms. Harris cannot be asked her opinion about the charges and what she wants as a verdict."

We argued about a few other things Winston wanted to have decided, but then it was my turn.

"Your Honor, I want to first deal with my client's prior record. He has two convictions from the State of Missouri, which score in this state as one count of second-degree burglary and one count of first-degree burglary. In this state, he has convictions for two counts of vehicular homicide. I would first ask the court to get the prosecuting attorney to declare whether he intends to offer any evidence of these offenses in the event Mr. Harris does not testify."

"Your Honor, I have no intention of introducing any of Mr. Harris' convictions, unless Mr. Cole finds some way to suggest to the jury that Harris has none."

"Your Honor, then I will focus on when, and if, my client does choose to testify. All but the two vehicular homicides are older than 10 years. Under the rule the court can make a finding that the interest of justice would be served by admitting evidence of an offense older than 10 years, but I would argue these offenses occurred when Jeff was seventeen and nineteen years old in a different state, involving none of the people in this case. With respect to the two vehicular homicides, they are sixteen years old; they are not crimes of dishonesty; and the tragedy that occurred was nothing Jeff intended."

"Mr. Cole," the Judge responded, "It hasn't gone without my being aware, that your client becomes 'Jeff' when you are appealing to my discretion. When you are talking in front of the jury, you will refer to him as 'Jeff Harris,' 'Mr. Harris,' 'Harris,' or 'the defendant.' With respects to your motion, something may happen to make any of the defendant's convictions admissible, but, Mr. Winston, you will need to ask my permission before you offer any conviction evidence."

"Next, Your Honor, I believe Mr. Winston may be planning to offer Mr. Harris' statement to Detective Gray. Judge Greenberg decided the admissibility of that statement. I am moving the court to order that Mr. Harris' statement that he might be going to jail be redacted. That might suggest to the jury that Jeff... Mr. Harris, has a criminal history."

"Your Honor, that goes to the defendant's motive; it shows the reason he was particularly angry with his wife."

"Mr. Cole, Mr. Winston is on strong ground; he can include that if he wants."

"Understood, Your Honor. If that is the case, I want to be sure that the whole statement gets presented. The evidence rules require that when the prosecutor offers a part of the defendant's statement, then the remainder of the statement must be read in fairness to the defendant.

"Counsel, that's not exactly what the rule states. It states that other portions, not necessarily the whole statement, must be introduced which 'ought in fairness be considered.' I'm going to wait until Mr. Winston makes his offer and decide then what else must be included."

At the completion of pretrial motions, Judge Tibbits asked everyone other than the parties and court staff to leave the court.

"Mr. Harris and Mr. Cole. I understand this is a three strikes case. Have you been offered a plea to something other than a strike offense?"

"Your Honor," said Winston, "we offered Mr. Harris a plea to solicitation to commit an assault two."

"Your Honor, that's right. "Mr. Harris would rather go to trial."

The judge turned to Jeff.

"Have you had a chance to talk about the prosecutor's offer with your attorney? Is there anything about the facts or the law of this case you don't think you fully understand?"

"No ma'am. . . Your Honor. I want my trial; I didn't do this."

"OK, bring in the jury panel."

With that, thirty jurors, wearing their numbered badges, walked into the room. Jurors numbered one through twelve sat in the jury box. The rest sat in order in the public seating. They all rose, raised their right hands, and swore to answer our questions truthfully. Judge Tibbits then introduced the case:

"Members of the jury panel, the title of this case is 'State of Washington verses Jeffrey Dwayne Harris.' It is a criminal case in which Mr. Harris is accused of the crime of second-degree assault by strangulation of his wife Darlene Harris."

The judge then introduced Winston and me, and, on cue, we each stood and turned to present ourselves to the panel. On the judge's invitation, I then introduced Jeff.

Following the introductions, the judge read the standard instructions advising the panel what their jury service involved and what their obligations would be if they were selected to serve. With the agreement of both sides, she released juror number Six who had a business trip scheduled for the next day, and she addressed a few general questions to the panel as a whole to assure, for at least her satisfaction, that they all could be fair. It then became the lawyers' turn to ask questions.

Hudson County has a quite diverse population. The majority live and work in urban or suburban areas, but a large minority live out in the farmlands or up in the mountains with occupations appropriate to those areas. Daily activities would not normally be bringing these groups together, but we were about to create a group of people from all these backgrounds and ask them to respectfully reason with one another in deciding upon a verdict in this case.

Prosecutors go first. It has always seemed to me their job in jury selection was easier than ours. Most people show up for jury service thinking the system generally works pretty well, and the guy in the defendant's chair wouldn't be there if there wasn't something to it. That's why the defense gets the "presumption of innocence" weapon. Winston seemed to spend his time trying to identify members of the panel who expressed disagreement with the thoughts of the rest of the group as potential candidates to be excused. He spent most of his time asking general questions to the whole panel and, as was common, there were a couple of the panel, jurors numbered Five and Nineteen, who loved to talk and offered their opinions on all his questions. Most of rest of the panel responded with a show of hands in agreement with what the speaking juror had said. I needed to know more about each person to make my challenges more effectively.

In response to Winston's question of whether they could follow the law, whether they agreed with it or not, Juror number Two announced she was willing to follow the law, until it conflicted with her own sense of what was right. This kind of independence suggested a level of thoughtfulness that could have been helpful to our side in the jury's discussions, and I was disappointed, but I had no reason to object, when she was excused.

It was then my turn. One of the objects of my questioning was to find and excuse members of the panel who themselves, or a friend or family member, had been a victim of domestic violence and likely to recast what happened in this case in the light of their experience. Jurors numbered Eight and Thirteen were quick to acknowledge that, based on their experiences, they didn't think they could be fair, and Judge Tibbits let them go.

I was also looking for those on the panel who tended to look at life in black and white terms and wouldn't be able to appreciate the subtleties involved in the events they'd be hearing about. As always, I was on the lookout for any jurors with an alpha personality. If one of them got into the jury room, the carefully considered thinking of each of the other eleven could be put aside for the conclusions of that one. And in my experience, alpha personalities don't walk into the court with the ability to appreciate the circumstances of all those little people they consider beneath them. From the answer he gave to Winston's questions and the fact that he was so insistent we hear him out, I was suspecting juror number Five might be a candidate. It's not that number Five wouldn't be fair, but what is "fair" to someone depends on what their life has taught them. With my admittedly biased preference, I've always preferred to have others decide the verdict. That is why lawyers have the power to make a limited number of what are called preemptory challenges, allowing them to remove a juror they don't think would be favorable to their case, even if the juror isn't legally disqualified from hearing it.

My approach to questioning is to ask a general question but to direct it first to a single panel member, and then to ask a couple others what they thought and finally to open it up to anyone who wanted to respond. In talking about the "presumption of innocence" and the requirement of "proof beyond a reasonable doubt" the members of the panel all spoke positively until I asked whether a five percent chance of rain led to a reasonable doubt of having a sunny day and then compared that to the question of guilt at which time the opinions diverged. My purpose was not to find agreement but to generate thoughtfulness in the deliberation.

With some premonition, I then asked that, given there would be no dispute that Jeff put his hands around his wife's neck, could they still carry the 'presumption of innocence' with them throughout the presentation of all the evidence and in their consideration of the two lawyers' final arguments. Jurors number Eleven and Twenty-one confessed that, with that evidence, they could not see any way they wouldn't be voting to convict. I always appreciate the honesty of people making that kind of admission, but to reinforce the "presumption" in the minds of the others, I asked the judge to excuse them for cause.

The judge gave Winston an opportunity to ask the two jurors some additional questions, and he got them to say that they would listen to all of the evidence, follow the law as given by the judge, consider what the lawyers said, and be fair. Back to me, juror number Eleven stated that, unless it was done as part of an act of invited affection, he would definitely be voting guilty. Juror number Twenty-one compromised a bit and stated he could keep an open mind. Juror number Eleven was excused for cause, but my motion to excuse number Twenty-one as well was denied.

When the questioning was completed, Judge Tibbits turned to Winston and me for our up to six preemptory challenges. As usual, prosecutors go first, and Winston challenged juror number Seven. My first challenge was, of course, juror number Five. Although he never said anything that would justify a challenge for cause, he had continued to answer to most of the questions in a way that made me think he had an alpha personality.

When jury selection begins, those numbered one through twelve are presumed to be the jury. If one of the twelve is removed because of a scheduling conflict or because they were excused for cause or on a preemptory challenge by Winston or me, the next numbered juror replaces that juror. So, Thirteen replaced Six; Fourteen replaced Two; Fifteen replaced Eleven; Sixteen replaced Thirteen (who had replaced Six); Seventeen replaced Seven and Eighteen replaced Five.

At this point, Winston declared he was satisfied with the panel. I had five more challenges I could make. The panel, as it was at that point, was acceptable to me, but I was hoping to get juror Nineteen into the jury. He was one of the two frequent volunteer talkers throughout the questioning, but unlike jury number Five, I thought he had some pretty thoughtful things to say. I wanted to get him onto the jury, so I challenged number Three even though she would otherwise be an acceptable juror for the defense, and she was replaced by number Nineteen. However, as I feared, Winston challenged number Nineteen before he even got out of his seat to enter the jury box, and he was replaced by number Twenty. Disappointed with the loss, I didn't think I could improve it for the defense, so I accepted the panel. When number Twenty-one became the alternate juror, having tried to get him excused for cause, I offered my challenge and number Twenty-two became the alternate juror.

When jury selection was complete, those selected stood and

swore to "well and truly" try Jeff's case, unaware they would be deciding his fate for the rest of his life.

Judge Tibbits put off opening statements until the next day but read the jury the standard introductory instructions before letting them go, including the requirements they not talk to anyone about the case or pay attention to anything that might be in the media.

The jail guards gave me a couple of minutes with Jeff after the jury, court staff, and prosecutor left the courtroom.

"Jeff, do you have any questions or is there anything else you want me to know?"

"I don't have any questions, but I've been thinking. I'd give my right arm, no, both arms not to have to spend my life in prison, but I know our society wouldn't agree to such a thing because it would be considered cruel and unusual punishment, whereas a three-strikes life sentence isn't."

I had no response except, "Jeff, I am just so sorry."

The jail guards came and took Jeff back to jail. I packed up and headed back to the office, hoping someone would be there and ready to get away for an earlier happy hour. It was nearing five o'clock, but the offices were alive with activity. I wasn't the only one in trial and most of the lawyers not in trial were there preparing for a trial just around the corner.

Sydney Johnson and Joyce Benson were game, and we managed to duck out and head to the usual pub across the street. We stopped for a quick chat with several of the court clerks seated in a booth celebrating the end of their day, then stopped by the bar to order beer and headed to the back for some privacy. Sitting there with Sydney and Joyce, I began to relax just a little. I had talked to both of these lawyers endlessly about Jeff's case from every possible angle, so it was time to talk about something else. Sydney started off on his favorite topic, national politics, with Joyce going toe to toe with him where she disagreed. Put either of them in charge of our nation and we'd be on a fast track to a better life for all. The beer helped, but I was still anxious about the next day, so I mostly listened. It was nice to be thinking about something other than my trial, particularly because the state of the nation was something pretty much out of our hands. Eventually, it became time to go home.

Again, I stayed up late thinking, and re-thinking about the trial. I had a fairly good idea how Jeff's testimony would go. We had been over it and over it together. I did not know for sure what Darlene was going to say. She loved Jeff, but she has been consistent with everyone that there had been one point with Jeff's hands around her neck when she hadn't been able to take a breath. I did finally get my head out of the trial and off to sleep, and the next morning I was ready to go.

CHAPTER FIFTEEN
Day Two

It was time for the two sides to make their opening statements. Lawyers are supposed to limit themselves to telling the jury what they believe the evidence will show and save their arguments for guilt or innocence until their closing. As with everything, prosecutors go first, and Winston kept to the proper script outlining what his witnesses would say. He concluded by saying: "Based on that evidence, members of the jury, you will find 'beyond a reasonable doubt' that Jeffrey Harris is guilty of the crime of second-degree assault."

Defense attorneys are often hesitant to make their opening statement at this point in the case, particularly when most of the defense case is a response to the evidence the prosecutor presents, and I was definitely feeling that hesitancy. I wasn't completely certain I'd want Jeff to testify and, although our pretrial investigation had given us a picture of Darlene's understanding of what happened, there were so many subtleties in what had happened that we could not be sure what exactly we were going to have to respond to. The defense can delay giving its opening statement until it starts presenting its evidence. But from day one, I'd been trained that, despite being instructed not to do it and without intending to, jurors start to draw conclusions at the opening bell. So, it's almost always best to take this opportunity to say something. I got up, stood before the jury, and told them about Jeff (using his full name) and Darlene, and their two daughters, Jenny and Christi. Then:

"Ladies and Gentlemen, this is a good family in a bad circumstance. They have been struggling with extremely limited resources and a tremendous debt. Jeff Harris had recently lost a good job as a diesel mechanic and, although Darlene Harris has a job, there was almost no cash on hand. To Darlene, it was necessary to spend some of what there was for shoes and a coat for their daughter Christi. When Mr. Harris found out she had done that without consulting him, he became angry. This is the sort of thing that can happen in any family. You will hear from witnesses this is not the kind of thing that is a feature of the relationship between these two people. Startled by her husband's anger, Darlene began to walk away. It was important to Jeff Harris that he explain to Darlene what she had done. Mr. Harris had set aside that money to pay a debt to the court with a fixed deadline. As Mr. Winston told you, he did grab her by the neck, but it was not to punish her, as he suggests, but to keep her in the conversation. At one point, Darlene tripped and fell to the floor; Jeff Harris let go of his grip but continued to try to tell her what she had done. Darlene ran out of the house to their neighbor. Mr. Harris did not pursue her; he remained in the house trying to calm himself and was there when the police arrived. Members of the jury, Jeff Harris never intended to cut off the flow of blood through his wife's neck or to obstruct her ability to breathe. You will see that and find him not guilty."

—

The first witness was Officer Fleming. He testified he and Officer Brown had been dispatched to the residence of Mary Jordan in response to a 911 call where they found Darlene upset and crying. Winston then asked the officer what Darlene told them. I thought about objecting because it was hearsay, but I knew Judge Tibbits would find it admissible hearsay because it was an excited utterance. Officer Fleming testified Darlene told him her husband had come home angry and yelling at her and when she turned to walk away, he grabbed her around the neck. Fleming then went on to testified he and Brown went to the Harris home and arrested Jeff. In line with Judge Greenberg's ruling at the pretrial hearing, Winston did not ask, and Fleming did not say that Jeff told them anything. On cross-examination, Fleming did acknowledge Jeff was completely cooperative with them during the arrest.

Mary Jordan was the next witness. She told the jury she had heard crying outside her apartment and, when she looked out, she saw her neighbor Darlene Harris very upset and crying. She testified she took Darlene into her apartment where she continued crying and said Jeff had grabbed her around the neck.

"Ms. Jordan," asked Winston, "did Ms. Harris say anything else happened to her during the time Mr. Harris had his hands around her neck?"

"Yes, she said she was choking and couldn't breathe."

"Thank you, Ms. Jordan.

"Your Honor, I have no further questions."

I started my cross-examination and, daring to do so only because I knew the answer from our investigator's interview with her, I asked: "Did Ms. Harris tell how long it was when Mr. Harris' hands were around her neck when she couldn't breathe?"

"Yes, she said it was just for a moment, but it had really scared her and that is why she ran out of the house."

On further cross-examination, Jordan told the jury that the Harrises were good neighbors, that she had often seen Darlene and Jeff playing outside with their two daughters, and she had not seen or heard of anything like this before.

Winston's first witness in the afternoon session was Detective Gray. She testified about the steps she took in the investigation of the case, including her interview with Darlene at her home the day after the incident. Winston did not try to offer what Darlene had said to Gray. It was not an excited utterance like the statements to Officer Fleming and Mary Jordan, but it would be available to Winston if Darlene deviated much from it when she testified.

I was a little surprised Winston didn't have the detective present the statement Jeff had given her that had been found admissible by Judge Greenberg at the pretrial hearing. In thinking about it though, I realized, by not presenting it, Winston had prevented us from keeping Jeff off the stand and relying instead on his words to the detective as the basis for our defense. Winston definitely wanted to get a chance to cross-examine Jeff, and the statement to the detective would be available in the event Jeff deviated from it.

Darlene was the next and, as far as I could tell, last of the prosecutor's witnesses. She looked very distressed as she walked into the courtroom and up to the witness stand. She was escorted by the prosecutor's witness assistant. Although we didn't know what advice she had been given, we knew at least she had been independently counselled by Ed Parks, the attorney the court had appointed to advise her. I was a little surprised he wasn't there, but, as it happened, about the time Darlene took her seat in the witness chair after swearing to tell the truth, Ed walked hurriedly into the courtroom, gestured to Darlene and sat down in the public seating.

Winston started off easily. He is an experienced trial attorney and knew the jury would insist that he be kind. In response to his questions, Darlene told the jury she and Jeff were married; they had two daughters, Jenny and Christi; and she worked for a janitorial service. As Winston began to ask about the incident, you could see her begin to shake nervously.

"Please tell the jury what happened on the afternoon of October 12th when the defendant arrived at home."

"Jeff was angry. He wanted to know if I knew where the money was, the money in his wallet. I told him I had taken it to buy Christi some new shoes and a coat at the Goodwill because she had outgrown her old ones."

"How did the defendant react?"

"He got really angry and started yelling. I couldn't understand what he was talking about. I got very frightened and started to back away. I'd never seen him like that. He is really a good man. We have had a wonderful life together."

"Ms. Harris," interrupted Winston, "please answer just my questions about the incident on October 12th. What did the defendant do when you started to back away?"

"He grabbed me around the neck and pulled me toward him. He kept talking about what I had done to him and to the family."

"Were you facing him or facing away?"

"I was facing toward him when he first grabbed me, but I turned around trying to get away."

By this time, Darlene was beginning to cry. The court clerk put a box of tissues within her reach and Darlene pulled one out to dry her eyes.

After a brief pause, Winston continued. "How long did he hold on to you?"

"I can't really tell, but when I think about it, it was only a few seconds."

"What happened then?"

"I kept pulling away. And then I fell forward and started choking. Jeff kept a hold of me as I fell, but when I got to the floor, he let go and I got up and ran out of the house and over to my neighbor Mary."

"What caused you to fall?"

"I don't know. I just found myself falling."

"Ms. Harris, was there ever a time while the defendant had his hands around your neck when you couldn't breathe."

"Yes, I started choking at about the time I fell."

"And at some point, you couldn't breathe?"

"Yes."

"Thank you, Ms. Harris. Your Honor, I have no further questions of this witness at this time."

Judge Tibbits looked over at Jeff and me. "Your witness Mr. Cole."

Jeff grabbed me by the arm and started whispering in my ear. I put my hand on his arm.

"Your Honor, would it be possible to have the afternoon break now? I need to confer further with my client."

"Very well. Members of the jury, we are going to take our afternoon recess at this time."

The jury went into the jury room, the judge and court staff went into chambers, and Jeff was led back to a holding cell. I picked up my notebook and followed.

I could see Jeff was really frustrated.

"I didn't stop her from breathing. You've got to get her to say that to the jury."

"Jeff, there is nothing we can do to undo what she has said. It is very clear that is how she sees what happened. She made it clear in her statement to Detective Gray she couldn't breathe, and she said it again when Maureen, our investigator, and I interviewed her. If she said anything different now, the prosecutor will be able to question her about any inconsistencies with her statement. Our story is that you did not intend to restrict her breathing and telling that to the jury is going to be your job."

Jeff and I continued to talk for the next few minutes, until the jail guards knocked, entered the cell, and led the two of us back to the courtroom. Darlene, who had left the courthouse during the break, followed us into the courtroom and sat in the public seating. All rose when Judge Tibbits entered. The judge directed Darlene to retake the witness stand and the law clerk escorted in the jury.

"Please be seated. Mr. Cole, you may cross-examine."

Jeff could have been right; maybe she would have downplayed the choking, but we knew that the prosecutor's witness assistant has been staying close to her and that the Child Protective Services had been considering intervening into her custody of her kids, making Darlene more likely to want to appear to be cooperating completely with the prosecutor. And Darlene's appointed lawyer had told us that she was not going to change her story. It had always been a possibility that Darlene would have tempered her testimony to help her husband. A couple of my colleagues had told me they thought that might happen. But my conversation with her that day at her dad's house led me to think she probably didn't feel she possessed the kind of privilege it would take not to be completely honest.

I started off. "How long have you and Mr. Harris known one another?"

"Ten years, we met when we were in an alcohol treatment program."

"You told the prosecutor you and Mr. Harris were living together at the time of this incident. How long had you been living together?"

"Nine years."

"You also told the prosecutor he is the father to your daughters Jenny and Christi. Has Mr. Harris been actively involved in parenting your daughters?"

"Oh, very much so, he is a great father."

"Does he love Jenny and Christi?"

"Yes."

"Does he love you?"

"Absolutely."

At that point, Winston objected. "Your Honor, this is not relevant."

I responded. "It goes to motive, Your Honor."

"I'm going to overrule the objection," said the judge, "but Mr. Cole, you need to move ahead."

I started again. "Ms. Harris, what is the state of your family's finances?"

"Jeff lost his job about three months before this incident, and we have been struggling ever since. We owe money to the doctor for when Jenny broke her arm. Jeff hasn't been able to pay his restitution, and we have been behind on our rent. As I told Mr. Winston, on the night of the incident, we were arguing because I bought some shoes and a coat for Christi at Goodwill with some of the money Jeff had put aside to pay some of our big expenses."

"Has an incident like what happened that evening ever occurred before?"

"No."

"Ms. Harris, directing your attention to the incident itself, you testified that at some point when Mr. Harris' hands were around your neck, you were choking and couldn't breathe. Was that the whole time he had his hands around your neck?"

"No."

"Was it a long time or short time?"

"A very short time."

"How many times when your husband's hands were around your neck did you try to take a breath but couldn't?"

"I have a clear memory of choking on one effort to breathe, but I was breathing clear right after that."

"You also testified you fell down at one point. How close in time was the fall to the time you couldn't breathe?"

"Just about at the same time."

"Your Honor, I have no other questions at this point."

"Any redirect, Mr. Winston?

Winston got up and walked over beside the jury box to draw Darlene's gaze directly at the jury.

"Ms. Harris, was there a period of time when Mr. Harris' hands were around your neck when your ability to breathe was being obstructed?"

Darlene answered, "For a very short time, yes."

Winston had gotten all he could, and her answers were all we could expect. Neither of us had further questions for Darlene. She was excused and left the courtroom with her appointed lawyer.

"We rest, Your Honor."

"Ladies and gentlemen of the jury, we have done a lot today, and although the day isn't quite over, I am going to let you go home at this time. I want to remind you that you are not to talk with anyone about this case. If anyone asks you about it, tell them the judge told you not to talk about it. You will be free to say what you want about the case when it is over. I haven't seen any reporters here, so you are not likely to see anything in the papers or on TV, but if you find anything in the media you are not to watch or read it. Have a good rest of the afternoon and evening."

The jury filed out, but Judge Tibbits remained on the bench. When the jurors were gone, I stood. "Your Honor, I have a motion for the court. Is this an appropriate time?"

"Yes, counsel."

This was the time when defense lawyers often ask the judge for a directed verdict of "not-guilty" on the claim the evidence the prosecutor had produced was not legally sufficient to support any verdict other than "not-guilty." Sometimes defense attorneys ask for a directed verdict as a matter of routine or even on the minuscule chance the judge would see a flaw in the prosecutor's case that even the defense attorney might not have seen. At other times, the motion gets vigorously presented. I had been debating to myself how to proceed in this case. The prosecutor certainly had shown Jeff had put his hands around Darlene's neck while angry, but at the same time, the restriction on breathing lasted only a second or less. If I took a vigorous approach, I didn't want to say anything that would expose a defense strategy we were planning to employ in the defense case or in closing argument that needed to be hidden until used. I had decided to give it all I had. Jeff's intent, which was going to be the major theme of my closing argument, was of no use here because in considering my motion, the judge would be required to consider the evidence so far in a light most favorable to the prosecutor. The evidence of Jeff's anger was certainly a basis upon which the jury could infer Jeff intended to strangle his wife. I had to go a different way.

"Your Honor, the defense moves the court for a directed verdict of not-guilty. Mr. Harris is charged with second-degree assault solely on the basis of the strangulation prong. The contact between Mr. Harris and his wife caused no injury and lasted only a moment or two. Any other kind of comparable physical contact between two people, be it a push, a grab, or a trip, would only be a misdemeanor if it were considered a crime at all. Looking at all the other things that constitute second-degree assault, such as substantial bodily injury, intent to torture, harming a mother with intent to injure her unborn child, I would argue that when the legislature added strangulation to this level of criminality, they did so envisioning something much more serious than what had occurred here. The definition of strangulation talks about 'obstruction of the person's blood flow,' and there is no evidence of that. The option we are dealing with is 'obstructing the person's ability to breathe,' but that really didn't happen here. What Ms. Harris said was that she choked in trying to take one breath. Your Honor, I would argue that does not constitute an inability to breathe. I ask the court for a directed verdict of not-guilty."

"Your Honor," Winston responded. "What the legislature did when they added the strangulation prong to the list of things that constituted second-degree assault was to make it as serious as substantial bodily injury and torture, and one of the major reasons for doing so was the use of strangulation in the growing problem of domestic violence which includes the very circumstance currently before the court. Mr. Harris may have only managed to hold on to his wife's neck for a short period of time, but, in that time, he did manage to affect her breathing, and even if the jury decided that Mr. Harris didn't accomplish a strangulation, the evidence would certainly support a jury finding that he intended to do so which also would constitute second-degree assault."

"Mr. Cole and Mr. Winston, we have an important question here, and I am going to give you an answer. However, considering what is at stake in this case, I am going to take the rest of today and this evening to consider an answer.

"Gentlemen, this case will proceed tomorrow without delay if I deny Mr. Cole's motion. Have a good evening."

—

The judge left the bench, the guards took Jeff back to the jail, and I went back to the office. Part of me had been hoping we could have finished the trial so I could breathe again, but the other part of me was happy to get out of the fight for a while. When I arrived, George Sanders came to my office to keep me company. However, although Jeff and I had been over his testimony from top to bottom several times, I knew I had to go see him before this incredibly important day in his life. I thanked George for handling those hearings scheduled for some of my other clients and I headed out.

—

It was late by the time I got to the jail, but the lawyer visiting facilities were still busy. I went to my assigned room and waited. When they brought Jeff in, I could see he was angry.

"I didn't strangle Darlene."

"Jeff, as a question of law, that is what I argued to the judge, and it is possible Judge Tibbits will agree with us and rule that the evidence of strangulation was insufficient."

"What would happen then?"

"Well, the prosecutor might proceed against you on a lesser charge, but there would be no life sentence. But Jeff, we have to stay focused because we are not going to get any time out if we lose the motion, and you are our only witness. We need to keep in mind that the jury is going to believe what Darlene told them, because she has no motive to hurt you, but what she said leaves us with some avenues of response. Darlene testified she was choking for only a truly short time and that was close in time to when she fell. When you testify, you are not going to contradict what she said. You can say you were not aware she was choking. But the central theme of your testimony has to be that you never intended to stop her from breathing or to cut off the flow of blood to her brain."

We sat there in silence for a few moments. Jeff stood up and I followed. I put my hand on his shoulder and we shook hands.

On my way out of the jail, Laura Berg caught up with me.

"Steve, how is your trial going?"

"We'll be done tomorrow. First thing, the judge is going to be ruling on our motion for a directed verdict. If we lose, the client will be testifying; then closing arguments."

"I hear this is a 'three strikes trial.' Didn't they make him an offer?"

"Yes, but it would still mean three years in jail and client said 'no'."

"Oh, God."

"Yes."

"What are your chances for a directed verdict?"

"Not so good. I was actually a little surprised the judge didn't rule against us right away. I just finished talking to my client and we are ready to go."

Laura invited me to go get a glass of wine with her. But I was under too much stress and just went home in the hopes of getting into my other world for just a while.

CHAPTER SIXTEEN
The Last Day

We had been called to appear at nine, ahead of the return of the jury to hear Judge Tibbits' decision on my motion for a directed verdict. The judge had not entered, and Jeff and I were sitting at our table when Winston came up to me and asked to talk in the hall.

"Steve, I am going to make you our offer one more time and offer to recommend the low end of the standard range for solicitation to commit second-degree assault. I had to push pretty hard for this and I will tell you I am a little more confident that I am going to defeat your motion than I let on."

"Thank you, Bob. I will see what Jeff says."

I went into the courtroom and asked for a short delay and a little privacy with my client. When the law clerk returned with the court's approval, Jeff and I were escorted down the hall to one of the conference rooms.

"Jeff, the prosecutor is offering to let you plead to the solicitation to commit—"

"I've already told you. No."

"Jeff, they are offering to recommend the low end of the range. Let me look it up quickly." I scrambled through my piles of paperwork for the answer. "Your sentence would be 31 1/4, more than ten months less than they were offering before. And with good time you'd be out in 21 1/2, less than two years."

With that, I had managed to slow down Jeff's responses, and he sat quietly for a few minutes. Then he asked me, "Is there a chance the judge will grant our motion for a directed verdict?"

"Jeff, there is a chance, but I think it is quite unlikely."

"If we go ahead with the trial, is there a chance the jury would find me not guilty?"

"Yes, the jury could vote to acquit, but this has always been an extremely tough case and the jury could very easily find you guilty. You know you can take the deal, be out in less than two years, and go ahead with the divorce you were talking about to cut Darlene and your kids off from that debt you owe to the court, if that's what's bothering you."

Jeff was silent, looked up toward the ceiling and took a heavy breath.

"I can't do that if there is any chance of winning, I am going to take the chance and not the plea offer."

I advised Winston of our decision, then knocked on the judge's door to let the court clerk know we were ready to go.

It wasn't long before Judge Tibbits took the bench. Some of the jurors had arrived and had been escorted to the jury room. The judge directed the law clerk to go to the hall to hold back other jurors who would be arriving over the next few minutes.

"Mr. Cole, I am denying your motion for a directed verdict. You had a strong argument for an acquittal of Mr. Harris, but it was dependent on questions of fact which I find to be questions for the jury to answer.

"I presume we are ready to proceed."

With that, the judge returned to her chambers and the arriving jurors were allowed to pass through into the jury room. There was nothing that needed to be said between Jeff and me, and it was clear he was deep within his own thoughts.

One of the jurors called to say he would be late because he was having to go get his mother to look after one of his kids who got sick in the night and had to stay home from school. There was nothing to do but wait, but it didn't help my nerves, and it had Jeff just shaking. In clock time, it really wasn't long before the juror arrived. We stood when Judge Tibbits entered the courtroom and remained standing until the jurors had entered and taken their places.

"Mr. Cole, you may proceed with your case."

"Your Honor, the defense calls Jeff Harris."

As Jeff walked to the witness stand, it went through my head how many times I had heard criminal defense lawyers advise against putting clients on the witness stand, even when the client has a good story to tell or is actually innocent. Testifying in court is a unique experience for a defendant during which they are going to be required to provide answers to precise questions from lawyers with carefully honed skills in getting the answers they want. Add to that the fact that there is so much at stake that a defendant's fear and anger can so often interfere with attending to the precise questions being asked or cause them to answer with an emotional response that undercuts what they were trying to say. In this case, however, Jeff had always said he wanted to testify, and, of course, that was his constitutional right. We had spent hours preparing him to testify and if he could make a strong presentation to the jury on the issue of what his intention was, our chances would be greatly improved.

Jeff took the stand, stood, and swore to tell the truth, then stated his "true name" and spelled it for the court record. I took Jeff easily through his first meeting with Darlene at the alcohol treatment program, how their relationship developed, their marriage, and the birth of their two daughters. He also testified about the desperate financial situation the family was in as a result of his loss of employment. So far, his testimony was going smoothly, but I could see him getting more anxious as we approached the incident.

"Mr. Harris, I want to take you now to the incident on October 12th. Your wife testified that when you came home that day, you were very angry. Please tell us, what had you so upset."

Jeff proceeded to tell the jury about his day in court on Monday, October 10th, when a judge ordered him to pay $50 or check into jail on Friday, the 14th. He described how he got the $50 in cash from his brother in the evening on that Monday, with plans to make the payment to the court the next day. I had hoped we wouldn't have to talk about his debt to the court or possible jail. Those are the kind of facts that can make jurors draw unfair conclusions. But Judge Tibbits had made it clear the prosecutor could use that part of Jeff's statement to Detective Gray, so we had decided to put it out there, in as positive a light as possible.

Jeff continued his testimony, telling the jury he didn't go to make the payment on Tuesday because he had an interview with a likely job offer that would start at the end of the week, so he went on Wednesday.

"But when I reached into my wallet to pay the cashier, the money wasn't there. I raced home to see if Darlene knew where the money was, and she told me she had taken it out of my wallet on Wednesday morning to go buy shoes and a coat for Christi. All my plans to get us back on track, pay the court, start that job, and start paying off our debts—ruined."

"Jeff . . . uh Mr. Harris, why did you grab your wife around the neck."

Jeff, looking right at the jury and shaking with emotion: "She wasn't listening to me and was backing away. I had to tell her what she had done to our plans to get out of the mess we were in."

"At any time, when you had your hands around Darlene's neck, did you intend to obstruct the flow of her blood to her brain or to prevent her from breathing?"

Breaking into tears, "No, absolutely not"

"Your Honor, I have no further questions, and I would ask if we could take a short break."

The judge agreed and the jury retired to the jury room. Jeff got down from the witness stand and came over to sit down with me.

"Jeff, that was ok. The prosecutor will be asking you questions next. Try to stay calm and remember to listen to the question. Ask him to repeat the question if you don't understand what he is asking. As we have discussed, he is going to ask you leading questions calling for just a 'yes' or 'no' answer. Be sure the wording he uses to pose those questions accurately reflects how you would answer those questions before you agree to answer 'yes.'"

It was a short break. The judge and jury were soon back in place with Jeff on the witness stand. Winston stood and began his cross-examination. After a few preliminaries, he began to focus in on the central issues.

"You came home to punish your wife because she had taken the money you needed to buy shoes and a coat for your daughter?"

"No, when I came home, I didn't know what had happened to the money. I wanted to know if she knew where it was. I was still hoping to find it and get back and make the payment."

Good work, Jeff, I thought. Winston wasn't able to lead you to where he wanted you to go.

"Ok," continued Winston, "when you got home and learned she had taken your money, you got angry at her."

"Yes."

That wasn't perfect. Jeff was claiming his rights to the fifty dollars. That would be something we would need to fix on re-direct.

"You became angry with your wife because now you were going to have to go to jail."

"Yes."

Jeff wasn't listening carefully, but then he hadn't been playing these lawyer games like Winston and I have.

"Have you ever been as angry with your wife as you were that day?"

"No"

"You choked your wife, because she took your money and that meant you were going to go to jail."

I could see Jeff was getting totally frustrated and becoming angry.

"I didn't choke my wife."

"You heard your wife tell this jury that there was a time when your hands were around her neck when she couldn't breathe. Was she lying?"

With his voice raised, Jeff was now losing control.

"No, she isn't lying, but she's got it wrong. I never stopped her from breathing."

"Mr. Harris, on October 12th of last year, you came home angry with your wife because she had taken your money, the money you were going to use to pay a debt to the court so you could stay out of jail. And that anger caused you to put your hands around her neck cutting off her ability to breathe."

"No, that's wrong, I didn't choke my wife; I love her."

"Your Honor," said Winston, sounding a little triumphant. "No further questions."

Jeff was so obviously emotional; I knew the judge would have given me a recess if I needed it. However, I didn't want the jury to think I had passed him a script for the re-direct.

So, I began, hoping Jeff would remember the things we had talked about.

"Mr. Harris, I want you to testify about what was going through your mind when Darlene told you she had spent the fifty dollars."

"I was upset because all I could think was that I was going to jail and be unable to take the job I had been offered."

"Were you just frightened about going to jail?"

"No, I've been to jail before, but I needed to go to work to be able to pay off our debts and support our family."

"What did you think of your wife using those fifty dollars to buy Christi those shoes and a coat?"

"I was angry with her; she had made a mistake. It was something we should have talked about. But it mostly made me realize what a failure I was. I couldn't even provide enough money to buy shoes and a coat for my child at the Goodwill."

"Why did you grab Darlene by the neck?"

"She was backing away, and I needed her there when I was feeling so low."

"Did you ever, in your time together that day, intend to obstruct the blood flow to your wife's brain?"

"No."

"Did you ever intend to choke her or obstruct her ability to breathe?"

"No, I didn't. She and our kids are the most important things in my life."

I had no further questions and Winston had nothing on re-cross.

"Your Honor, the defense rests."

It was close enough to the lunch hour, so Judge Tibbits excused the jury and took the opportunity to talk about jury instructions, the directives she would read to the jury prior to the presentations from the lawyers. Most of what the judge had decided to present were the standard instructions identifying the specific elements that make up the crime and the procedures the jury had to follow in deciding whether those elements had been proven. The prosecutor and I had each proposed instructions when the trial began. and were now going to find out what the jury would be told. I was relieved the judge agreed to give the jury the option of the lesser crime of assault in the fourth degree. If the jury decided Jeff did assault Darlene but didn't intend to strangle her, they could find him guilty of the lesser crime and then the judge could only sentence him to 364 days in jail, much of which he had already served waiting for his trial.

The case was now ready for closing arguments. I left the courthouse and went down to the river to escape the turmoil for just a few minutes and to review one more time what I was going to say. The time went by fast, and we were all soon back in court. Each juror was given a copy of the instructions, and they read along as the judge read them aloud. Closing arguments were next, and Winston stood and approached the jury.

Winston was an experienced prosecutor. He had to prove "beyond a reasonable doubt" that, as a result of Jeff's hands around her neck, even if just for a moment, Darlene was unable to breathe. There was no doubt; Darlene had given him that. What he also had to show was that Jeff intended to cut off her breathing. That was going to be harder, but he had several things to argue, and he made the most obvious point first.

"The defendant claimed to you that he grabbed his wife around the neck so he could continue 'telling her' what she had done. You could accept that if the story was that he grabbed her by the arm, by her shoulder, or by the tail of her coat. But you don't stop someone from walking away from you by grabbing them around the neck. The defendant put his hands around his wife's neck in order to strangle her."

Winston made several other arguments, including one that surprised me, claiming that Darlene fell during the incident because the choking had caused her to lose consciousness. I was going to have to deal with that, but I already had a different scenario in mind.

"It's also important to keep in mind," he went on, "that this wasn't a conversation between a husband and wife. This was the defendant venting his anger at someone who had taken his money, which he was going to use to keep himself out of jail."

I objected. "Your Honor, the prosecuting attorney is distorting the facts."

"I am going to overrule the objection; this is closing argument and some leeway is allowed. However, Mr. Winston, this was close; you need to be sure to stay within the bounds of legitimate argument."

Winton continued. "What is important here is not what the money was to be used for, but the defendant's extreme anger at his wife for taking it when he needed it so badly. Anger is not a time for conversation; anger is a time to do something to the person or thing you are angry at. This is not a crime that requires premeditation. To be guilty, Mr. Harris didn't have to have a plan to assault his wife when he walked in the door. It could have been a momentary decision on his part, one he may have immediately regretted. The defendant did obstruct his wife's ability to breathe and, maybe only briefly, he did intend to do that. What you have heard these past two days establishes beyond a reasonable doubt that Jeffrey Dwayne Harris is guilty of assault in the second degree as he was charged."

Winston sat down and Judge Tibbits invited me to begin: "Mr. Cole."

The most important part of my presentation was going to deal with those terrible moments, but I started off reviewing for the jury what they had learned about the Harrises. It was important to show Jeff as a human being living in a human world. I reminded the jury about the evolution of Jeff and Darlene's relationship from their meeting as patients at an alcohol treatment facility, through the nine years of their marriage, including the birth and parenting of their two daughters. I underscored what Darlene had said, that there was no history of violence in their relationship, and this was the only incident of its kind.

Winston's argument that Darlene's fall was the result of her passing out was something I had not anticipated. I decided I would deal with that next.

"The prosecutor suggested to you that Darlene fell because she had been choked to the point of unconsciousness. That is simply not consistent with the testimony you heard. If Darlene had passed out, she would have told you. What she did tell you is that, when she fell, she immediately got up and ran to the neighbor's house. She didn't spend any time lying on the floor recovering from being unconscious. Actually, it is much more likely that the choking she experienced right at the time that she fell occurred, because in falling her head jerked forward causing an unintended compression of her windpipe."

It was now time to get to the core of our case.

"Members of the jury, Mr. Winston has argued Jeff must have intended to choke his wife because the single focused thought of anyone who is angry is to strike out at the object of the anger. That is a very simplistic view of anger and not one that accurately describes Jeff's mind at the time of this incident."

I realized I had started referring to Jeff by his first name, but this was closing argument and the judge hadn't said anything, so I decided to continue doing it.

"Jeff admitted he was angry with Darlene, but he also described how he was angry with himself for putting himself into that fix and for failing to be able to get the job that would let him provide for his family financially.

"It is also an over-simplification to look at the emotion Jeff was feeling as just anger. When a person gets emotional, there is almost always more than one element in that emotion. In Jeff's case, he was angry with Darlene and with himself, but there was also his frustration at the circumstances he was in and his shame, embarrassment, and despair over the future for his family. With all those emotions in play, Jeff wasn't trying to hurt Darlene. He needed her close to help him handle the complex emotions he was feeling and to face the difficult future ahead."

I spoke briefly about the lesser crime option, but I didn't want to spend much time there, afraid the jury would take it as an admission Jeff had committed an intentional act.

In the last chapter of my closing, I talked about "the presumption of innocence" and the requirement of "proof beyond a reasonable doubt" in the instructions the judge had given them.

"Members of the jury, the evidence you have heard in this trial has not overcome the presumption of innocence and leaves you with many reasons to doubt, that Jeff intentionally strangled his wife. What began two days ago as a presumption of innocence ends today with the reasonable conclusion that the choking which Darlene Harris experienced was an untended accident. When you have carefully considered all the instructions that Judge Tibbits read to you and looked closely at all the testimony, you will see that the only just verdict is not-guilty."

I was done and couldn't help beginning to feel some relief. Winston got another turn talking to the jury and there was nothing I could do about what he said, unless he went beyond responding to what I had said.

Winston knew the rules, and he focused his argument on trying to get the jury back to the idea that Jeff's anger against his wife was the single thing in his mind. He didn't talk long, and the case was then in the hands of the jury.

Judge Tibbits had decided to send the jury home and have them start deliberations the next day. She carefully instructed them not to talk to family members or friends about the case and to stay away from the local news until they were discharged by the court after reaching a verdict.

—

With the trial completed for the day I went back to my office intent on figuring out which of those things left undone I had to tackle first, but when I got there I found I had no energy and started packing up to go home. When they heard I was back, Howard Graham, Rachel Pierce, and Eric Scanlan stopped by my office and were soon joined by Anita Carter and the boss, Jill Zimmerman, all wanting to know how things had gone.

"Well, there were no happy surprises," I had to admit. "The wife gave the prosecutor what he needed, that her ability to breathe had been restricted. Jeff testified really well, and we are just hoping the jury can accept the idea that an emotion filled with anger and frustration doesn't necessarily include an intent to hurt someone."

I hadn't stopped to notice during trial, but several the public defender lawyers had stopped into our courtroom when they had a break to watch the proceedings.

"I watched the wife's testimony," said Rachel, "and was a little surprised that she didn't lie about what happened or at least hedge a little bit."

"We didn't expect anything different. She had told her neighbor she had been choked and said the same to the cops, making it clear to them she couldn't catch a breath. CPS has also poked its nose in and appears to be ready to seek supervision of her custody of her daughters if she does anything to help the 'bad guy.'"

Anita had watched Jeff's testimony.

"I thought your client testified pretty well. I was looking at the jury's reaction. They were all being attentive to his testimony, but there were no smiles or nods suggesting acceptance of what he was saying."

I got several compliments about my closing argument, and I appreciated hearing them. However. coming from my colleagues at the high point of my trial anxiety, I think of it more like a pat on the back than a real critique.

—

I told everybody I had a date with my wife and had to get out of there. That was no lie. I'd been an absent husband and father for the last couple of weeks, and my wife Stephanie and my kids Tyler and Jessica had cornered me that morning as I was about to leave for court and ordered me to take them out to dinner. I drove home weary, worried I wouldn't be a very responsive member of the party. But when I pulled into the driveway and my wife and kids piled into the car, my energy seemed to return. On the drive to the restaurant, Tyler and Jessica started talking about things— what was going on at school and what their friends were up to. These conversations continued through dinner. Jessica told me all about her dance class and Tyler proudly showed me his essay from school with a big red A. Stephanie had a couple of stories about some funny things the kids in her class had done. From lots of experience, they all knew the rule, and there was not one word spoken about my case. My thought about Jeff and our case did return to me when I handed my credit card to the waiter to pay for our dinner. What was such a simple thing for me would have been impossible for Jeff, and there was no reason to think his family was entitled to any less joy than mine.

It was past the kid's bedtime when we arrived home and we hustled them through the evening routine. Exhausted from the ongoing tension of the day, I was in bed shortly after them, but not before Stephanie and I agreed the two of us would cut out for a weekend very soon.

CHAPTER SEVENTEEN
The Verdict

It was nine o'clock in the morning and I was back in the office. Nine o'clock was the time Judge Tibbits had instructed the jury to be back in court to begin deliberation. I knew there wouldn't be a verdict for a while, but the idea that those twelve people had begun their work was a little chilling. I did my best to concentrate on the pile of files on my desk. One of the advantages of being in trial is that, in your head at least, you get to relieve yourself of all those other responsibilities. However, once you have finished a trial, even if you are still waiting for a verdict, all those responsibilities come crashing back.

There was a trial scheduled in two weeks and the investigator had left me an email that he had interviewed the store owner who had been robbed. There was a motion to suppress evidence, and I needed to do some legal research to empower my claim that the police officer didn't have 'probable cause' to arrest my client. And there were those three new cases I knew nothing about that I needed to get started on.

I stopped by Polly's office to collect her list for me and a recommendation for where to start. She gave me a pre-verdict hug, and I spent a few minutes giving her the highlights and lowlights of the case as I saw them. As I backed out of her office, we signaled each other with crossed fingers in both hands. I did pretty well all morning focusing on the projects Polly had listed for me, but after lunch I couldn't escape thinking that after three hours of deliberation Jeff's jury would be coming back soon and I lost my ability to concentrate.

At about two in the afternoon, the call came from the court. The jury had reached a verdict. Jeff was in the jail, and it was going to take a little while to get him changed into his court clothes and over to the courthouse. I had plenty of time, but with the verdict in, I couldn't think of anything else, so I stopped to pick up Maureen and Meredith, and headed over to wait as long as it took. Somehow, word got out at HPCD that there was a verdict, and a large contingent of the lawyers and several of the staff were not far behind us. Winston's colleagues had heard the news as well, and he was there with a number of other prosecutors when we arrived. Darlene and the witness assistant were there too. It seemed like we waited quite a while, but finally, escorted by two more guards than there had been for the trial, Jeff walked in and sat beside me. It surprised me, but he seemed to be at peace. The law clerk looked out from the judge's chambers and, seeing everyone had arrived, stepped right back in to inform the judge. The court staff came out and took their places and almost immediately we heard the order to stand and Judge Tibbits entered.

The judge ordered the jury to be brought in. We remained standing while the jurors came in and stood at their respective positions in the jury box.

"Please be seated."

With everybody settled, Judge Tibbits looked over at the jury and asked the presiding juror if the jury had reached a verdict.

"Yes, we have, your Honor."

The law clerk picked up the verdict forms and handed them to the judge. The judge read them to herself and handed them to the court clerk. These formalities always seem to take too long, but the consequences attached to this case made it particularly hard to endure.

The court clerk received the verdict forms and read:

"We the jury find the defendant Jeffery Harris guilty of the crime of assault in the second degree."

I dropped my head and closed my eyes, and for a moment all I could sense was my heart beating fast. I looked over at Jeff, still looking at peace. I think with the ratio of the good and the bad things that have happened in his life, he had assumed all along it would be a guilty verdict. I put my hand on his shoulder.

"Jeff, I am so terribly sorry." The two of us turned around and could see Darlene silently crying. I looked over to where my colleagues were seated. Looking back at me, Maureen raised and dropped her hands, signaling her exasperation at the verdict.

We sat down and the judge continued her dialogue with the jury to be sure that all twelve members agreed, thanked them for their service, and asked them to return to the jury room.

When the jurors were out of the courtroom, Jeff spoke.

"Your Honor, we know what the sentence is. Would you just impose it and let me get out of here?"

Winston said he had the paperwork all ready and was willing to proceed, but I objected.

"Your Honor, I have to be sure that there has been no stone unturned; I need at least a week."

"Your Honor, I object," said Jeff, staring at me angrily.

"Mr. Harris," said the judge. "I am going to set out the sentencing at least a week, not because your lawyer is asking for it, but because I want to be sure I am doing the right thing."

"Your Honor," I asked, "I have another request. I would like you to strike the no-contact order between Mr. Harris and his family. There are a lot of things this family has to figure out."

Winston objected.

"Mr. Harris has just been convicted of committing domestic

violence against his wife."

I responded: "Ms. Harris' job as witness has been completed and the State's need to protect that from possible interference no longer exists. There is no evidence of other physical or psychological abuse by Mr. Harris against Ms. Harris beyond this incident and the Harrises love each other. Whether it be done at the jail or from her home, their conversations will be safely over a telephone, which Ms. Harris can just hang up at the first sign of anything she doesn't like."

Winston capitulated, but only for the week between then and the sentencing. The judge thought that was fair and lifted the no-contact order for the following week. She ordered the jury released and declared the court in recess.

Everyone in the public seating but Darlene and her witness advocate quickly cleared the courtroom, at which point the jail guards stepped up to take Jeff back to jail. Darlene was crying as they led him away. When he was gone, she got up and walked out too.

At that point, the law clerk opened the door to the jury room, and the jurors filed out. Winston and I stood at our desks as they walked by. For the most part, the jurors were not interested in talking to us. However, the presiding juror did stop and say that the jury had agreed Mr. Harris had done something very wrong but asked me to tell him he had a nice family, and all the jurors were hoping he could find a way to get back together with his family again when he finished his prison sentence. I thanked her for her comment and said no more.

Maureen, Meredith, and several of the HCPD lawyers were waiting outside the courtroom and urged me to join them at the pub, but I declined. Instead, I walked quickly back to my office, dumped off my trial notebooks, and went home.

———

During the week between the verdict and the day for the sentencing, there was much to do. I went to the jail a lot. I had several new clients to see so I could get started on their cases and to apologize for not seeing them sooner. Polly had also given me a long list of the clients in cases already underway. Most of them were in jail, some of those wanting to try to get their bail lowered, others just wanting to have more contact with their defense team. There were some requests from clients who were out of custody too, but nowhere near as many. Even though many of these clients are facing consequences as serious as those in custody, being out of custody permits them to be less focused on their cases. We can live with that so long as they do show up at their next court hearing. As we frequently remind our clients, most of what we do for their defense is done outside their presence: reading the police reports and the witness statements the police had obtained; conducting our own witness interviews; researching the exact meaning of the law; and writing briefs assembling that research to support the claims we make in court. I spent a lot of my week catching up on this work as well.

Even though there appeared to be no alternative to the life sentence without parole for Jeff, we spent considerable energy looking for one. "We" included me of course, but also several of the other lawyers who had volunteered to help, each of them agreeing to think as creatively as they could to try to find the yet-unknown path under, around, or over the three-strikes wall. Eric Scanlan, with his prior appellate work, contacted some of the appellate lawyers he had worked with for any ideas they might have. Nothing! We all ended up at the same place, the Washington State Supreme Court opinion of State v. Witherspoon, where the sentencing judge said he didn't think Alvin Witherspoon should be sentenced to life without parole but imposed the life sentence nevertheless because he found that the law required it, and the

Supreme Court, in a five to four vote agreed with that.

We were definitely going to file a motion requesting the court to enter a "judgement of acquittal notwithstanding the verdict." Seeing how focused the issue was in this case and remembering how Judge Tibbits had responded to essentially the same motion at the end of the Prosecutor's case, we did not think there was much of a chance of winning, but it would give the judge an avenue, if she wanted it, to avoid giving Jeff the life sentence. The most important part of our presentation to the court was going to be Meredith's social work report, but we also decided to fill the record with messages from everyone one who knew Jeff. We got letters from Darlene and her father Mike Houser, and a beautiful note from Jenny. Brother Bill and a fellow diesel mechanic wrote supporting letters as well. Even Detective Joyce Gray, who had interrogated Jeff, while not offering an opinion about the sentence, did write about the profound remorse Jeff had expressed during his interview. All these communications were provided to Judge Tibbits in advance of the hearing and filed in the court record for appellate purposes.

—

With that work completed or underway, I needed to meet with Jeff. I decided to take Maureen whose witness interview were such a big part of our case. Jeff was waiting in the interview room when we arrived.

"I am glad you guys came over; I wanted to thank you in private for what you tried to do for me. It was a tough case, and you left nothing undone to try to help me."

"Jeff, I want to tell you what we are going to be doing from here. We have a social work report by Meredith Hayward attacking the level of your guilt for your prior convictions, particularly the burglaries, because of your age at the time those crimes were committed and several letters supporting you that are being sent to the judge; Darlene and her dad and your brother, and even Jenny, wrote one. And-- "

Jeff interrupted. "What for? You have told me many times there is only one sentence for a three-strikes case."

"Jeff, you're right. Judge Tibbits is not likely to do anything else, but we want this all on the record for the appeal."

"I'm not going to appeal. I took my chance and lost. I am ready for a life in prison. Darlene can't be waiting around for me; she needs to move on, as we have discussed. And even if you got me a standard range sentence, I'd still be doing the kind of time I'd have done with the plea bargain I turned down. No, I don't want to appeal."

"A couple of things. We need to appeal the conclusion that what you did constituted 'strangulation' as it was envisioned by the legislature when they made it a class B felony that qualifies for a three-strikes sentence. We also want to challenge the three-strikes law because it is a bad law, and we need the facts of your case and your life and how you have lived it to show that everybody who gets three-strikes isn't a fundamentally bad person who needs to be in prison for life to protect society.

"You took the risk to try to get out now so you could get back to building a life for your family and you lost. Now, with your plan to divorcing Darlene, putting her in a far better financial position and, as you were hoping, in a place where she could find another partner to help give her and your kids a better life. But that still doesn't mean you have to stay in prison all your life. If you can get out in three years, five years, or ten years, you wouldn't have any more responsibility for Darlene's family. You'd still have to pay your $50 a month to the court and wouldn't be able to buy a house or get a cheap loan, but you'd be free, which might even include some kind of relationship with Darlene and your daughters.

"It's also important that we appeal your case as a tool for

attacking the three-strikes law for all the other men and women, some of whom will spend the rest of their lives in prison, and others, unlike you, who would give up their right to a trial and a claim of innocence and plead guilty to a prosecutor's plea offer to avoid the risk of the life sentence."

Jeff sat for a while, looked over at Maureen, up at the ceiling, then at me.

"Alright, we can appeal."

"Jeff, there is one other thing. You have what is called the right of allocution, the right to speak to the judge prior to the imposition of sentence. The law doesn't require you to speak, but I would ask you to think about having something to say. If you do say something, you should definitely include what you have been arguing all along, that you never intended to strangle Darlene."

"I will think about that, thank you."

It was time to leave. I signaled for the guards; Maureen and I stood and shook Jeff's hand; the guards came and took him away; and Maureen and I went back to the office.

—

Later that afternoon, I was just beginning to do some legal research for a pretrial motion in another case, and Jill Zimmerman came to my office.

"Steve, I wanted to stop by to see how things were going. I've been a little worried about you, with all the pressure you have been under these last few weeks."

"Thanks Jill, I've been worried about me too."

"I know you worked really hard on the Harris case, and all reports from people in the office confirm that you did a wonderful job. I watched your closing argument and thought it was an effective presentation. I know you were disappointed in the verdict. We all were. But you can't let what those twelve people decided be your measurement of what you did."

"I've never experienced this much pressure in my work here as with this case. It wasn't overly complicated but getting to know Jeff and his wife and family, against the background of the life sentence we were fighting, made it really hard. What really helped though, were the concerns expressed by so many people in the office."

"Yes, Jeff, I've always thought of HCPD as bunch of team players engaged in what ends up as a non-team sport."

—

We were all in place in Judge Tibbits' courtroom waiting for her to come out and take the bench. Jeff and I sat at one counsel table, Winston and Chief Criminal Deputy Pamela Berens sat at the other. In the front row of the public seating were Darlene with Christi in her lap and Jenny seated right beside her. Her appointed lawyer Ed Parks was with her, but she had managed to persuade the witness assistant they were no longer needed. Also seated in the front row were the elected prosecutor Cantrell and Detective Gray, and Maureen our investigator and Meredith our social worker. Seated in the rest of the front row, the rest of the public seating, and all available standing room were a large contingent of HCPD lawyers and staff, a substantial number of lawyers and staff from the prosecutor's office, a couple of reporters and two members of the jury. The chambers door opened, and the court staff came out and took their places. The law clerk stood.

"All rise, Department Four of the Superior Court of the State of Washington, in and for Hudson County, is now in session, Judge Jennifer Tibbits presiding."

Judge Tibbits walked in. "Please be seated," she said, and everyone took their seat.

"This is the case of the State of Washington verses Jeffery

Dwayne Harris. The first item for consideration is the defense motion for a Judgement of Acquittal Notwithstanding the Verdict. Mr. Cole, I have read your brief and the response from the prosecuting attorney. Is there anything additional authority you would like to present?"

"Your Honor, I have no additional authority. It is our position the State did not present sufficient evidence to prove Mr. Harris intentionally compressed Darlene Harris' neck in a manner that obstructed the flow of her blood or her ability to breathe or that he grabbed her around the neck with any such intention. Mr. Harris was only holding onto his wife so he could continue to talk to her. In support of this motion, we have submitted numerous letters from people who know Jeff... Mr. Harris, including his wife and other family members, and Detective Gray, who is here today, all demonstrating that Mr. Harris is not the kind of person who could do something like that to his wife."

Winston stood to talk, but the judge held up her hand. "Mr. Winston, I don't need to hear from you. Mr. Cole, I don't believe that anyone's reputation among friends and family members could ever foreclose a situation like this one where a person gets so angry they act outside of their character. The issue for the jury was straightforward and I must let their verdict stand."

Disappointed but not surprised, I move on to deal with the no-contact order.

"Your Honor, the defense is asking the court to make permanent the lifting of the no-contact order between Mr. Harris and his wife and children."

"Based on all of the supporting letters and the request of Ms. Harris," said the judge, "I am inclined to permanently remove the no-contact order. Mr. Winston, does the State have anything beyond what was stated on the day of the verdict?"

"No, your Honor."

"Then I will grant the request of the defendant and that of his wife to lift the no-contact order without any prejudice against it being re-imposed at a later date. Let's move on to the sentencing. Mr. Winston?"

"Your Honor, I am handing to the court what have been marked as State's Sentencing Exhibits one through four. Exhibit 1 is a certified copy of a judgment and sentence from Carter County Missouri showing a conviction of Jeffrey Harris on one felony count of what qualifies in Washington as second-degree burglary. Exhibit 2 is a certified copy of a judgement and sentence from Shannon County Missouri showing a conviction of Jeffrey Harris on one felony count of what qualifies in Washington as first-degree burglary. Exhibit 3 is a certified copy of a judgement and sentence from Adams County Washington showing two convictions for vehicular homicide while under the influence of intoxicating liquor. Exhibit 4 is a statement sworn under penalty of perjury from a certified fingerprint expert attesting to the fact that the fingerprints on exhibits 1 through 3 matched Jeffrey Harris."

Winston continued. "Exhibits 2 and 3 establish that the defendant has been convicted of two crimes designated as most serious offenses. His conviction in this court of second-degree assault constitutes a third conviction for a most serious offense. The only sentence the court can impose is life in prison without the possibility of parole."

Judge Tibbits looked over to me. "Mr. Cole?"

"Your Honor, it is the position of the defendant that a life sentence would violate the Washington State and United States constitutions by denying Mr. Harris his right to due process and his right to be free from a punishment that would be unconstitutionally cruel and unusual. Given the nature of Mr. Harris' offense, we ask that you impose a sentence of two months with credit for time served. Has the court received and considered the sentencing memorandum and the supporting letters submitted by the defense?"

"I have received them and read them carefully. They are a part of the record of this sentencing."

That was good to hear. The purpose of our presentation that day was not just to persuade Judge Tibbits, who probably didn't think she had the authority to impose a sentence other than life, but also to try to persuade the state and federal appellate courts. Her agreeing that she had read the letters made them part of the record.

"Your Honor, we would like to call one witness, Darlene Harris."

"Proceed."

Darlene stood, placed Christi in the seat next to Jenny, walked to the witness stand. At my request she read her letter to the court in which she described the history of her relationship with Jeff.

She concluded: "Your Honor, I love Jeff; he is the anchor for my life and for the lives of our daughters. He did not intend to hurt me and does not deserve to spend his life in prison."

Our presentation completed, Judge Tibbits invited Winston to respond.

"Your Honor, none of this matters. Mr. Harris made his choice when he decided to take this case to trial. The court is required to impose a life sentence without the possibility of parole."

"Mr. Harris," said the judge, "is there anything you would like to say to me before I impose sentence?"

Jeff stood and read his presentation. He told the court about his regret about those days as a wild kid when he committed those burglaries for the excitement it brought him and his buddies, and about the terrible loss of his friends in that horrible car crash for which he experiences guilt every day of his life. He told the judge about the turnaround that began while serving that sentence in prison and how his life was brightened when he met Darlene and how his nine years with her and with their daughters has been the highlight of his life.

"Your Honor, I never intended to strangle my wife."

"Thank you, Mr. Harris. Sir, I have listened to your allocution; I have listened to your wife's testimony; I have read the defense sentencing memorandum and all the letters submitted on your behalf; and I have listened to your lawyer's argument. However, I am not going to consider the teenage immaturity that helped to lead you into committing those burglaries in Missouri; I am not going to consider the depth of the guilt, that I know you have, over the homicide of your friends; I am not going to consider the nine crime free years you spent putting your life back together after your release from prison; I am not going to consider the love you brought to your wife Darlene, and your daughters Jenny and Christi. No, I am not going to consider any of these things because the law is very clear as to what your sentence must be and none of that matters.

"Jeffery Dwayne Harris, I hereby sentence you to life in prison without the possibility of release.

"This court is in recess."

I sat there beside my client without the energy to move. Once the verdict was in, everything was telling me this was how it was going to end, but it still struck hard when I heard the judge make it a reality. I couldn't help but think what Sydney would be saying—that for Jeff and I, Darlene, Jenny, and Christi, Winston, and Judge Tibbits, and even the jury—this had been a situation where the law had absolutely required us to become involved in a really stupid and futile gesture.

EPILOGUE

The story of the Hudson County Public Defenders is finished. The purpose of this epilogue is to show the reader who is interested in looking deeper, how Washington State criminal law has evolved over the years, how the laws work, and how they would have been applied in the cases handled by the Hudson County Public Defenders.

Up until the early 1980s, felony sentences in Washington and many other states were imposed on an individualized basis. The sentencing judge made an independent decision on the basis of the injuries and damage done in the commission of the crime and the character of the person being sentenced for the crime. The judge could either impose a jail sentence of a year or less together with probation, where the defendant remained responsible to the judge. Or the judge could send the defendant to prison for a term specified in the law for that crime. From there the actual time served in prison and any conditions upon release would be set by the parole board again on the basis of the injuries and damage done in the defendant's criminal career and the defendant's character and any accomplishments while in prison.

All of that was changed in the Sentencing Reform Act of 1981. Today the sentence ranges—the range of time from which the judge selects for the defendant to serve in prison or jail—is found on a grid arranged along its vertical axis according to the seriousness level and along the horizontal axis according to the defendant's offender score. The seriousness level of felony offenses is established by statute. The defendant's offender score begins with the category of crime for which the defendant is being sentenced: violent offense, non-violent offense, sex offense, etc. Using the rule for that crime category, each of the defendant's prior offenses is scored as a 1, 2, 3, or 1/2 [3] depending on the category of the prior offense. The total number of points is the defendant's offender score and, together with the seriousness level of the crime, determines the sentence range. Once the sentence range is determined, the judge, in all but exceptional circumstances, will select a number of months or days from that range.

One of the central reasons for this change was to prevent any social bias from playing a part in felony sentencing. It did limit the discretion of the sentencing judge, but it did nothing to stand in the way of the prosecutor bias in deciding what crime to charge or what plea bargains to offer.

Incarceration rates in Washington have gone up dramatically under the Sentencing Reform Act.

---

[3] A 1/2 is the score for a non-violent offense committed by a juvenile.

Here is the grid at Washington law number RCW 9.94A.510.

	Offender Score Seriousness Levels									
	0	1	2	3	4	5	6	7	8	9
Level 16	Life in Prison Without the Possibility of Parole									
Level 15	240 - 320	250 - 333	261 - 347	271 - 361	281 - 374	291 - 388	312 - 416	338 - 450	370 - 493	411 - 548
Level 14	123 - 220	134 - 234	144 - 244	154 - 254	165 - 265	175 - 275	195 - 295	216 - 316	257 - 357	298 - 397
Level 13	123 - 164	134 - 178	144 - 192	154 - 205	165 - 219	175 - 233	195 - 260	216 - 288	257 - 342	298 - 397
Level 12	93 - 123	102 - 136	111 - 147	120 - 160	129 - 171	138 - 184	162 - 216	178 - 236	209 - 277	240 - 318
Level 11	78 - 102	86 - 114	95 - 125	102 - 136	111 - 147	120 - 158	146 - 194	159 - 211	185 - 245	210 - 280
Level 10	51 - 68	57 - 75	62 - 82	67 - 89	72 - 96	77 - 102	98 - 130	108 - 144	129 - 171	149 - 198
Level 9	31 - 41	36 - 48	41 - 54	46 - 61	51 - 68	57 - 75	77 - 102	87 - 116	108 - 144	129 - 171
Level 8	21 - 27	26 - 34	31 - 41	36 - 48	41 - 54	46 - 61	67 - 89	77 - 102	87 - 116	108 - 144
Level 7	15 - 27	21 - 27	26 - 34	31 - 41	36 - 48	41 - 54	57 - 75	67 - 89	77 - 102	87 - 116
Level 6	12+ - 14 [4]	15 - 20	21 - 27	26 - 34	31 - 41	36 - 48	46 - 61	57 - 75	67 - 89	77 - 102
Level 5	6 - 12	12+ - 14	13 - 17	15 - 20	22 - 29	33 - 43	41 - 54	51 - 68	62 - 82	72 - 96
Level 4	3 - 9	6 - 12	12+ - 14	13 - 17	15 - 20	22 - 29	33 - 43	43 - 57	53 - 70	63 - 84
Level 3	1 - 3	3 - 8	4 - 12	9 - 12	12+ - 16	17 - 22	22 - 29	33 - 43	43 - 57	51 - 68
Level 2	0 - 90 days	2 - 6	3 - 9	4 - 12	12+ - 14	14 - 18	17 - 22	22 - 29	33 - 43	43 - 57
Level 1	0 - 60 days	0 - 90 days	2 - 5	2 - 6	3 - 8	4 - 12	12+ - 14	14 - 18	17 - 22	22 - 29

---

[4] Felony sentences of a year or less are served in the county jail, a year or more in prison. The use of 12+ makes it clear that any sentence imposed within this particular range would be served in prison.

To illustrate the complexity, assume a defendant comes before a judge for sentencing. Their criminal history includes one sex offense and one felony theft. If that defendant were being sentenced for theft of a motor vehicle, a Level 2 offense, their offender score would be 2 and their sentence range would be 3 to 9 months. If the same defendant were now being sentenced for second degree rape of a child, that prior theft would continue to count 1 point, but the prior sex offense would count 3 points. The offender score would now be 4 and the sentence range for a Level 11 offense 111 to 147 months.

—

Cindy Baker was charged with first degree trafficking in stolen property, a level 4 crime. If she had been convicted, her sentence range with a zero-offender score would be 3 to 9 months. Her plan to become a nurse would have to have been put off for at least 5 years, if not permanently.

Gilbert Martin was originally charged with second-degree robbery for stealing groceries from Safeway by force when he threatened the two employees who came after him. The robbery charge is also a Level 4 offense. Gilbert had one prior felony, a second-degree theft, so his offender score was 1 and his sentence range would have been 6 to 12 months in jail. He pled guilty and was sentenced to a lesser offense of fourth-degree theft, which was a gross misdemeanor, not a felony, so his sentence was not determined on the grid. The judge had the authority to sentence Gilbert to between 0 and 364 days.[5]

Ray Langus was sentenced for a felony, second-degree robbery, the same crime Gilbert was charged with, a Level 4 offense. The two other robberies that had him in prison each counted two

---

[5] Several years ago, Washington reduced the maximum sentence for a gross misdemeanor by one day to 364 days to avoid certain immigration consequences.

points in his offender score because they are classified in the law as violent crimes. With an offender score of 4, his sentence range this time around was 15 to 20 months in prison, which would be served concurrently with the time already imposed in the prior sentence.

Lori Lucas was charged with first-degree criminal mistreatment, a Level 10 offense. If she had been convicted, her sentence range with a zero-offender score would have been 51 to 68 months.

Walter Chandler's sentence was the most complicated. Walter had no prior felonies, so his offender score started out as a zero. As Sydney and Steve discussed, the Legislature changed the sentence range for second-degree rape twice. It started in the 1980s as a Level 9 offense. For a defendant with an offender score of zero, the sentence range was 31 to 41 months. In the early 1990s, it was changed to a Level 10 offense, with the sentence range of 51 to 68 months for a defendant with a zero-offender score. When it was changed again to the Level 11 offense it is today, the sentence range Walter was facing was 78 to 102 months.

Walter finally pled and was sentenced for the crime of third-degree rape, which is a Level 5 offense. With a zero-offender score the sentence range was only 6 to 12 months. Sydney knew that prosecutor Beth Wilkerson and crime victim Sandra Glenn would not have accepted that, so he proposed a legal fiction where Walter would also plead to some additional counts of third-degree assault. Two counts of third-degree assault would give Walter an offender score of 2 and a sentence range of 13 to 17 months. Wilkerson quickly refused, so Sydney offered a third count of third-degree assault that would give Walter an offender score of 3 and a sentence range of 15 to 20 months.

Wilkerson refused that as well, but countered with third-degree rape plus three counts of third-degree assault, each of the assaults with a designation of sexual motivation, which now as sex offenses counted 3 points. This gave Walter an offender score of 9 on the third-degree rape and a mandatory sentence of 60 months, the maximum sentence for third-degree rape.

Although that sentence only took off 18 months from the sentence Walter was facing for the original charge of second-degree rape, it foreclosed the involvement of the Indeterminate Sentence Review Board (ISRB) which, with a sentence for second-degree rape, could have extended Walter's sentence beyond whatever the judge set. The 60-month sentence Walter received for his felony offenses was the maximum he could receive for the lesser crimes of third-degree rape and third-degree assault, leaving the ISRB with nothing they could do.

Joe Sellers was convicted of second-degree assault, a Level 4 offense, the same Level of offense as those charged against Cindy Baker, Gilbert Martin, and Ray Langus. Joe had one prior felony theft conviction which counted as 1 point and that other assault conviction, the one the prosecutor wanted to admit into evidence at his trial, which counted 2 points because it was a violent offense. Joe ended up with an offender score of 3 and a sentencing range of 13 to 17 months in prison, and Judge Jordan gave Joe the high end of that range, probably because of the shenanigans he tried to play.

———

Jeff Harris' sentence was not a product of the sentencing grid, but it is worth making some comparisons. Because the death penalty has been determined to violate the Washington State Constitution, life without the possibility of parole is the only sentence available for adults for the single Level 16 offense of aggravated first-degree murder. Aggravated first-degree murder can be charged for multiple premeditated murders or a single premeditated murder under specified circumstances, including murder of a police officer or murder for hire. Jeff's sentence matches the sentence for aggravated murder. A first-degree murder that is not aggravated is a Level 15 offense. A defendant with no criminal history would be sentenced within a range of 240 to 320 months, which amounts to 20 to 26 2/3 years[6], around half of the 45 years Jeff would expect to live out his life in prison. A defendant being sentenced for a new first-degree murder who had a prior first-degree murder committed together with a second-degree kidnap would have an offender score of 5 and a sentence range of 291 to 388 months which amounts to 24 1/4 to 32 1/3 years.

Jeff was offered a plea bargain where the charge would be amended from straight second-degree assault to solicitation to commit second degree assault, a legal fiction considering what had actually happened, but a crime that no longer qualified as a strike. This offense would have been scored as a Level 4 offense, the same as for second-degree assault, but the number of months would have been reduced by 25%. Jeff's offender score would have been 7, 2 each for the two vehicular homicides and the first-degree burglary from Missouri, and 1 for the second-degree burglary from Missouri. The sentence range on the grid of 43 to 57 months would be adjusted to 32 1/4 to 42 3/4 months. The prosecutor's plea offer required that Jeff agrees to the high end. If Jeff had accepted that offer, he would have been released with one third off for good time after 28 1/2 months. The prosecutor's mid-trial offer to the low end would have made his good time release 21 1/2 months.

The sentencing grid does not play a part in the operation of the three strikes law. Very simply, there is a list of crimes that are strike offenses, officially called "most serious offenses." The list includes all of Washington's most serious Class A felonies and a list of lesser felonies, most of which are sex offenses, but also includes second degree assault. If a defendant had been

---

[6] There would be an additional three years for a person committing a murder with a deadly weapon, five years with a firearm.

convicted of multiple strike offenses in the past, it wouldn't necessarily make a new strike a third strike. To receive a life sentence, a defendant must have committed one strike offense, been sentenced for that offense, then committed a second strike offense and been sentenced for that offense and then committed a third strike offense.

Many real people in real Washington prisons who did not commit rape or murder, or trafficking in children for sexual purposes are, nevertheless, serving the three-strike sentence that Judge Tibbits handed down to Jeff.

BIBLIOGRAPHY

Missouri State Law

Burglary in the First Degree: section 569.160 RSMo 2017
Burglary in the Second Degree: section 569.170 RSMo 2017

Washington State Law

Assault in the Second Degree: RCW 9A.36.021
Assault in the Third Degree: RCW 9A.36.031
Assault in the Fourth Degree: RCW 9A.36.041
Attempt to Elude a Pursuing Police Vehicle: RCW 46.61.024
Criminal Mistreatment in the First Degree: RCW 9A.42.020
Driving Under the Influence: RCW 46.61.502
Persistent Offender (Three Strikes) RCW 9.94A.570
Possession of a Stolen Firearm: RCW 9A.56.310
Possession of Stolen Property in the Second Degree (credit card):
    RCW 9A.56.160
Sentence for Sex Offenders: RCW 9.94A.507
Rape in the First Degree: RCW 9A.44.040
Rape in the Second Degree: RCW 9A.44.040
Rape in the Third Degree: RCW 9A.44.060
Residential Burglary: RCW 9A.52.025
Restitution: RCW 9.94A.753
Robbery in the Second Degree: RCW 9A.56.210
Solicitation: RCW 9A.08.020(3)(a)(i)
Strangulation: RCW 9A.04.110 (26)
Theft in the Third Degree: RCW 9A.56.050
Trafficking in Stolen Property: RCW 9A.82.050
Uniform Rendition of Accused Persons (Fugitive): RCW Chapter
    10.91

Unlawful Possession of a Firearm: RCW 9.4.040
Vehicular Homicide: RCW 46.61.520

Washington State Court Rule

SID Standard 3, Caseload Limits and Types of Cases, Standards for Indigent Defense, 2013.

Washington State Sentencing Guidelines

Implementation Manual, Sentencing Guidelines Commission State of Washington, 1989.

Implementation Manual, Sentencing Guidelines Commission State of Washington, 1992.

Washington State Adult Sentencing Guidelines Manual, State of Washington Caseload Forecast Counsel, 2018.

Court Decisions

Gideon v. Wainwright, 372 U.S 335 (1963)
Miller v. Alabama, 567 U.S. 460 (2012)
State v. Witherspoon, 180 Wash.2d 875 (2014)

Other Sources

Bogira, Steve, *Courtroom 302*, New York, Vintage Books, 2005

Mayeux, Sara, *Free Justice, A History of the Public Defender in Twentieth Century America*, Chapel Hill NC, University of North Carolina Press, 2020

Rapping, Jonathan, *Gideon's Promise, A Public Defender Movement to Transform Criminal Justice*, Boston, Beacon Press, 2020.

Stevenson, Bryan, *Just Mercy, A Story of Justice and Redemption*, New York, Spiegel & Grau, 2015.

My Cousin Vinny, Dir. Johnathan Lynn, 20th Century Fox, 1992, Film.

National Lampoon's Animal House, Dir. John Landis, Universal Studios Inc., 1978, Film.

"FY2019 Cost per Incarcerated Individual per Day – All Facility Cost," Washington State Department of Corrections, 2019

LaCourse, Jr., David, "Three Strikes, You're Out: A Review," Washington Policy Center, 1997, washingtonpolicy.org.

"Less Guilty by Reason of Adolescence," McArthur Foundation Research Network on Adolescent Development and Juvenile Justice, adjj.org.

Sawyer, Wendy, "How much do incarcerated people earn in each state," Prison Policy Initiative, 2017, prisonpolicy.org.

ABOUT THE AUTHOR

Bill Jaquette practiced law for over forty years. During that time, he served as a deputy prosecuting attorney and was also in private practice. A substantial part of his career, however, was as a public defender, including thirty years with the Snohomish County Public Defender Association, of which he was also director.

In addition to his JD from the University of Washington, Bill holds a PhD in philosophy from the University of Missouri and, prior to his career in law, served as a tenured member of the philosophy faculty at Southwest Missouri State University.

Gideon's Grandchildren is his first novel.